Donita
Miller

Michelle

Eva Gibson

WHOLESOME READING DISTRIBUTED BY:

CHOICE BOOKS

IRWIN, OHIO 43029

We Welcome Your Response

Michelle

Eva Gibson

BETHANY HOUSE PUBLISHERS
MINNEAPOLIS, MINNESOTA 55438
A Division of Bethany Fellowship, Inc.

Other Springflower Books

Lisa, by Betty Shaffer

Melissa, by Eva Gibson

Michelle
Eva Gibson

Library of Congress Catalog Card Number 83-72409

ISBN 0-87123-405-X

Published by Bethany House Publishers
A Division of Bethany Fellowship, Inc.
6820 Auto Club Road, Minneapolis, Minnesota 55438

Printed in the United States of America

For my new daughter,
Shannon

EVA GIBSON is a homemaker and mother of six children. She is active in a Baptist church in Sherwood, Oregon, where she teaches Sunday school. She is a free-lance writer whose articles have been published in several youth periodicals. Her article in *Moody Monthly* was "Evangelizing Today's Child." She has also written personal-experience articles for *Counselor, Power for Living* and other Sunday school papers. Her first book was *Melissa* (Bethany House, 1982).

Contents

One / On the Banks of Eagle Creek

Mickey might have been a sculpture carved atop the gray boulder. Her silky hair lay dark against the April sky, her deep green sweatshirt distinct from, yet blending with, the barely budded alders.

Beyond her quiet figure, the creek flashed and roared and rippled and spit fine white spray. Then it changed—swirling, glinting—the quieter pools along the edges reflecting sky and trees, hinting at life deep within its depths.

"You dear, majestic, wild creek," Mickey murmured. "You're so alive—so vibrant. I'd like to get to know you ... find out why they named you Eagle Creek."

She hunched forward on her sun-drenched rock; a slight girl, with dark hair framing a small, heart-shaped face, with her dark eyes dreamy, her thoughts caught away in the music of the stream. She lowered her hand into the icy water.

He spoke from behind her. "Seen any fish?"

Mickey whirled around, her hands spraying cold

drops onto her jeaned legs. Her eyes flashed with momentary fear, reflecting something of the creek's mysterious depths.

But it was only a smiling young man who stood behind her, a fishing pole in one hand, a tackle box in the other. He was encased to the waist in heavy rubber boots, making Mickey wonder how he'd crept up so softly.

But it was his hair that caught her attention and kept her eyes riveted on him. It was reddish-brown and curlier than any hair she had ever seen.

"Seen any fish?" he repeated.

"No," Mickey mumbled, "not that I know of."

In one quick jump he cleared the water between the bank and Mickey's broad boulder. He looked at her with open curiosity and gestured toward the pink house behind them. "Friends of the Middletons?" he asked.

"Not exactly," she said. "I'm—I'm living there—"

"Really?" Surprise edged his voice. "Then you must be in our school."

Mickey squirmed uncomfortably. "I'm not in school," she said.

The young man shook his head. "You could have fooled me."

"I'm only sixteen," Mickey countered. "I haven't graduated—"

There was another long thoughtful look from the young man. But he didn't ask any more questions. Instead, he smiled.

"I'm Joel Brentwood. Kent lets me come and fish here anytime I want to, but I live in Estacada."

Mickey relaxed visibly. "That last little town you go

through before you get here?"

He nodded. "I'll be a senior in high school next year. I come up here as often as I can and fish. There's just something about this creek—" He broke off suddenly. "Do you fish?"

"No."

Enthusiasm lifted his chin. Mickey looked at him intently. *His eyes are that unusual strange color between gray and green*, she thought. *Like mother's were—*

Joel laughed out loud in obvious delight. "I'll teach you, whatever your name is."

Mickey smiled. "It's Mickey."

"Mickey?"

She nodded. "Just Mickey." Words suddenly tumbled out. "My real name is Michelle Ann Strand. But when I was little, everyone called me 'Mickey.'" She wanted to add, 'except my mother,' but she didn't.

"Mickey," he said tentatively. "Mickey. It's different—but I like it."

"I'm a ward of the court now," she volunteered. "Kent and Loretta Middleton are my new foster parents. I've never lived in the country before. It's always been the big city—"

"Wow!" He gestured toward the rushing water. "Well, how about it? Want me to show you how to fish?"

Mickey nodded. "Sure."

Joel put his tackle box beside her. "May I?"

Mickey peered inside. There were hooks, spinners, plugs and dainty flies of every description. She touched a rainbow-hued one gently.

Joel reached for a hook, ignoring the alluring flies.

He uncapped a jar of pink salmon egg clusters. "Right now those biggies out there are taking eggs," he explained, nodding toward the creek. "Yesterday I got three on. Brought one home, too."

He waded out into the water, his waist waders changing the pattern of the rushing creek. *He's tall,* she thought, *his curly head would even be above Kent's.* Joel flicked his wrist, and his line drifted into the middle. He looked back at Mickey.

"Go up to the house," he invited, "and ask Loretta for a pair of these." He patted his boots. "They've got lots of poles, too. Kent would be awfully glad to see you fishing." He nodded toward the house. "They all fish — even Loretta."

A deep excitement stirred inside Mickey. *Oh, to be out there in the middle of that wonderful rushing creek . . .*

She jumped to her feet, leaped across the small rocks and ran up the bank. She scurried to the basement entrance, pausing only long enough to take a deep breath of the heavenly white blossoms foaming over the giant cherry tree planted there. Then she was inside, up the stairs, and into the kitchen. "Loretta, could I learn to fish?"

Loretta turned, a slow smile widening her mouth. "Why, Mickey. That would be fine." She wiped her hands on a paper towel, a pleasant, attractive woman with soft dark hair tied back with a narrrow black band.

"We've got lots of extra equipment downstairs. I'll set you up." She led the way into the daylight basement room that served as a family room. Her eager voice trailed behind. "We're a fishing family, you know. Living on the creek like this, it's sort of expected, I suppose."

She opened a door at the bottom of the stairs. Mickey peered past her. An assortment of boots tumbled on the floor, poles lurked in corners, various jackets hung from hooks, as did a pair of long boots dangling on suspenders.

"You'll need these, now," Loretta explained, handing the boots to Mickey. "The rain we've had this spring raised the creek." A frown creased Loretta's face as she reached for a pole. "Someone will need to show you—" she said doubtfully.

"It's all right," Mickey interrupted. "There's a Joel somebody down on the rock. He has eggs and everything. He said he'd show me—"

"Oh—our Joel. That's great. Run along and have fun." She started up the stairs.

The big boots flopped awkwardly across Mickey's arm and bumped against her knees as she hurried down the slope. But the pole in her hand felt smooth and good, almost as though it belonged there.

She leaned it against the big rock and clambered up. "I got a strike!" Joel called. "But he's gone! Put your boots on!"

Mickey watched him as he turned and waded toward her. Even in the water his movements were free and easy, held in by a quiet controlled vitality. He smiled at her and she flushed. Awkwardly she pulled on the tall boots.

"They're too big!" she laughed, holding the floppy sides.

Joel agreed. "It won't matter though," he said.

"They'll keep you dry."

Carefully he selected an egg cluster and baited her hook. Together they waded into the icy stream, the water pushing against their legs, filling Mickey with a strange excitement. But the pole that had felt so graceful on the way to the creek suddenly seemed like an over-sized pencil, stiff and awkward.

"I'll help," Joel volunteered. Gently he rearranged her hands around the rod. Mickey threw her shoulders back and made a perfect cast. It drifted over the riffles and sank into a shady pool.

"All right!" Joel exclaimed. "There's fish there, too. I saw them, down deep—big steel gray—" He waded away from her down stream. "Just watch—"

He cast again, a long graceful arc, and the line shone silver. Mickey's pole quivered, the line suddenly taut. But it was only a submerged branch firmly attached. She hung tight while Joel came back and handed her his rod.

"It's one of the hazards," he explained as he set her line free.

Mickey was undaunted. She cast again, but this time her hook caught in the alders over her head.

Somehow she was caught off-balance and thrown to her knees. The creek filled her huge boots and pulled her downward—down—down—

Dimly she heard Joel shout, "Don't panic!"

But she did. The icy water rushed over her head, the weight of the boots welding her beneath the gushing stream. Cold terror froze her thoughts. She released the pole and grasped blindly for something to hold onto.

Joel's hands were on her shoulders, yanking her up into the blessed air. She gasped, clawing at his shirt.

Through a film of water she glimpsed fear on his face. Then she screwed her eyes shut and hung on. Together they stumbled to the shore.

"I'm so sorry—" she whispered. "I should have been more careful—"

Then they were beside a big rock. Mickey let go of his shirt. She clung to the rock's sun-warmed edge.

"Get rid of those boots," he advised. Mickey's icy fingers fumbled with the suspenders on her shoulders. She pushed off the heavy rubber and sat down abruptly, shivering. Joel got on his knees and began pulling off her boots.

Then with his soft flannel shirt in his hand, he was wiping her face. Mickey looked at him through drenched lashes and tried to smile. Trembling, he took the shirt and rubbed her dripping hair.

There was an angry shout from the bank. "Joel!" Mickey and Joel turned.

Kent stood there, a tall, lean, angry man, his legs stiff and braced apart. "Didn't you know better than to let her go out so deep? She could have drowned!"

Joel got to his feet and went toward Kent. But Kent paid him no attention.

"Go inside, Mickey!" he shouted. "We don't want a sick kid around here!" Abruptly, without another word, he wheeled away.

Mickey stared after him in shocked amazement. "His pole," she whispered in sudden consternation. "It's gone—" She shivered.

"Don't worry," Joel muttered. "I'll find it—if I can. Just go in and get dried out." He gave her shoulder a gentle shove.

Her sweatshirt clung clammily to her body as she stumbled up the bank toward the house. Loretta met her at the door, a bathrobe and towel in her hand, worry clouding her gray eyes.

"He's awfully angry—" Mickey faltered. She touched Joel's flannel shirt still draped around her dark mop. Great shivers ran through her body. Loretta reached for the edge of her sweatshirt and helped her wriggle out of it.

"Try not to be upset," she said.

"But why—why should he lash out like that at Joel?" she asked between the chattering of her teeth.

Pain etched lines into Loretta's face. "We've had a drowning—" Her voice faded. She pushed the robe into Mickey's hand. "Take off those soggy jeans and take a hot shower," she advised, nodding toward the bathroom adjoining the family room. "Come up when you're dry."

She turned abruptly and went up the stairs. Mickey looked after her. *Why had that haunted look suddenly masked Loretta's face? Why had Kent gotten so angry over a simple mishap? He'd been peaceable enough when she met him—except—except—*

The kitchen had been warm, scented with simmering meat when she'd first seen him. He'd been sitting at the kitchen table, a newspaper spread before him.

He had smiled as Loretta put her arm around Mickey, pulling her toward her husband.

"This is Kent," she had said, her gray eyes dancing. "He thinks all girls are special. Even shy ones with big, dark eyes like yours."

Kent had smiled. He had started to reach for Mickey's hand, then drew back. He had scowled, turning abruptly to Loretta. "Why don't you show her to her room? I'll mix the cornbread if you like."

Mickey had felt shattered. *He doesn't like me,* she thought. I wonder why—

As she had followed Loretta through the living room, she'd comforted herself by thinking, *But Loretta does. She said so.*

Even as Loretta opened the door, Mickey had sensed her change . . . .

Mickey pushed her memories aside and undid the flannel shirt wrapped around her head. For a moment she buried her face in its damp softness.

As she did, another dark thought shot through her. Had someone they loved been dragged beneath that cold, icy water? Loretta had said, "We've had a drowning." Mickey shivered and hurried into the bathroom.

Two / "They Don't Want Me!"

"I don't like this room," Mickey mumbled, "and it doesn't like me." She sat down on the edge of the pink ruffled bedspread and reached for her tennis shoes.

"It really doesn't fit this family," she continued, tying her laces. "And neither do I."

She pulled out a pair of blue jeans and a warm turtleneck sweater from the dresser. She put them on, her eyes examining the room's details: the pink ruffled curtains just matched the dressing table and spread, complementing the deep pink carpet, and a ballerina lamp reigning over a dainty flaring doilie. Even in the picture over the bed, white kittens with pink bows shouted, "Fragile, handle with care!"

How strange for an outdoor country family to have a room like this, she thought. "They should have done it in earthy colors to go with the rest of the house—and the outdoors," she decided aloud. "Not hot pink carpet with pale pinks and white."

She combed her hair into a semblance of order and drifted into the living room. Now here was a room! Plain

18

beige drapes were drawn back to reveal greening leaves, the foaming, rushing stream—the great blossoming cherry tree.

Creamy wallpaper with light etchings of green ferns climbed the walls, and big stuffed chairs and scattered cushions carried an invitation to curl up and enjoy the gifts of the great outdoors. And that was just what Steve Middleton was doing.

Sprawled in a corner chair, surrounded by scattered comic books, his blue-gray eyes regarded her solemnly. He nodded toward the window. "I saw you out there."

Memories of those icy rushing waters brought goose bumps out on Mickey's arms. She shivered.

"You almost drowned," Steve added.

Mickey's chin jerked. "Not really. It wasn't even over my head—and I can swim."

Steve shook his head. "It holds you down," he said.

Mickey shrugged. "So? But I didn't drown, did I?"

She plopped into a chair and regarded him curiously. Since she'd arrived at the Middletons' she'd seen little of Steve. After school he slipped through the house like a shadow.

Even at meals he kept his chin down, his eyes averted. His conversation was mostly, "Pass the milk, please." "Thank you." "Excuse me."

But something sparkled in his eyes now. Mickey smiled at him, gesturing at the scattered comics.

"Do you read a lot?"

He nodded, his thoughts quite obviously not on his books. "You sure got Dad upset."

Mickey squirmed uncomfortably. "I don't understand that. I never meant to."

"He gets like that when he's scared," Steve observed wisely. "He wasn't even thinking of you, not really."

"Not thinking of me! I was the one under the water!" Mickey spluttered. "What do you mean?"

But that hooded look covered his eyes again. He looked at his opened book and turned a page.

Dinner that evening was a solemn affair. Kent avoided meeting her eyes, and Loretta had little to say. If it hadn't been for Steve, Mickey was sure she wouldn't have been able to eat a bite. Somehow her afternoon episode seemed to have changed his attitude toward her.

His blue eyes regarded her curiously over the steaming stew and hot biscuits. "You look like you never fished before," he observed.

Mickey shook her head.

"Did you like it?

"I—I—Yes, I did, or at least I think I will after I've had more practice."

"The creek will close to anglers in a few days," he said, "but you can practice casting where the little trees are planted. That's what I did."

An uncomfortable silence followed. Mickey determinedly buttered her biscuit and took a bite. Steve looked up, caught her eye, and grinned encouragingly.

Mickey looked from Kent to Loretta, but both were concentrating on their food, Kent dishing up another bowl of stew and Loretta poking at a potato, a slight frown creasing her forehead.

Afterward, Mickey helped Loretta with the dishes, then went to her room. But its fragile, pristine beauty repelled her. She wanted to be outside, to absorb all the warmth she could out of the frail spring sunshine.

But as she stepped out of the frilly pink room, her eye was caught by a door to her left. It was slightly recessed and she hadn't noticed it before. Curiously, she opened it and saw steep narrow stairs yawning before her. She fumbled for the light switch, but no light beamed when she turned it on.

Funny, she hadn't thought about there being an upstairs in the house. But there was a door at the top of the stairs. She could see its vague outline in the uncertain light.

She went up slowly, her footsteps cautious on the uncarpeted treads. She tried the door, but it was locked. The knob firmly resisted her efforts.

Why would anyone keep an inside door locked? Mickey wondered. She tried to turn it again, but it coldly refused to move.

Mickey ran down the stairs, through the living room, and out the front door. Already the sun had disappeared behind the trees, and the air was cooling.

She reached the edge of the lawn and turned. Sudden excitement throbbed through her. The upstairs window at the back of the house was partially obscured by the cherry tree branches—but it faced the creek.

What an aerie! What a retreat, with the creek to rush and roar beneath you, and the cherry tree, that great white-blossomed giant right outside the window!

She ran her fingers through her dark hair, wondering if Loretta would let her unlock and explore the room. Memories of Loretta's and Kent's preoccupation at dinner made her doubtful.

Mickey raced across the grass. High above her

stretched the great branches of the cherry tree. She grabbed one of the lower branches and vaulted into the crotch of the tree.

She looked up. The top curled over her like a white canopy. She took a deep breath and exulted in the blossoms' subtle sweetness. High above her head the upstairs window seemed to beckon.

"I'm coming, I'm coming," she whispered. She clasped the tree trunk with one hand and, with the other, reached for a limb above her head.

Branch by branch she mounted higher in the tree. She paused and looked down. Everything looked different: the tops of the barely greening snowball bush, the rosy pink of flowering quince and the tiny dandelion gold studding the lawn. Across the yard the birch swirled tender new leaves, announcing in its own way spring's debut.

Mickey climbed higher. When she was across from the window, she inched forward on the limb. The bark pushed against her stomach and she lay cat-like, peering through the glass.

There was a bed with a bright-colored Indian blanket, a round multi-colored rag rug and a plain maple dresser. "Ooh," she murmured, "it looks so cozy. I wonder . . ."

"Mickey!" Loretta called. "Mickey!"

Mickey opened her mouth to answer, then shut it determinedly. Climbing fruit trees had been firmly forbidden by more than one foster parent. A picture of Kent's dark anger made her shiver.

Carefully, she backed along the branch until she reached the comparative safety of the inner branches, which were shaped like a pair of bird wings. She smiled and eased into them, her back comfortable against the warm bark.

For a moment she dreamed of her room—open window facing the tree, creek roaring its music day and night. She could have friends, too, in that aerie. She wasn't sure what they'd look like, but she could see their hazy outlines—one in the middle of the bright Indian blanket, the other cross-legged on the rug. A sweet sadness rose in her throat.

"A place of my own," she murmured, "a place of my very own."

She'd been saying that for as long as she could remember.

Her earliest memory transported her to a faded yellow house with a big porch. Her father honked the horn and they started off with a jerk, boxes and baggage rattling. Tucked in the back of a station wagon with her two brothers, she turned and watched the only home she'd ever known fade away.

After that came a jumbled succession of curtainless kitchens, battered linoleum and Kevin's crib shoved in any handy corner.

"A place of my own." She said it or thought it every time she stepped into a new house. It had been on the tip of her tongue when she'd arrived at the Middletons four days ago. She was saying it again now—

She looked down. The surging water seemed to beckon. She smiled, remembering Joel. There had been something about his eyes. They were like the stream— no, more gentle, kind. She wondered if she'd ever see him again.

A door below her closed. She looked back at the window and muttered, "I shouldn't—but I am."

Once again she inched along the limb. The window was close. Tentatively she released her hold on the branch and touched the ledge. Cautiously she slid forward, the branch still firm beneath her. Her hand met the window glass. She pushed. The window opened and Mickey scrambled inside.

The room was all she had dreamed and more. It was L-shaped, and the half she hadn't seen through the glass boasted a desk and another window. Mickey opened it and leaned far out. The stream's voice and the fresh scent of firs mingled their welcome. She caught her breath.

"I'm home! I'm home!" she exulted. She drew in her head and did a quick whirling dance in the middle of the room before collapsing on the rug.

She looked around. Knotty pine slanted across the sloping ceiling. Paneling of the same kind covered the walls. A closet door, slightly ajar, invited her scrutiny.

Mickey jumped up and opened it wide. A jumble of empty jars, books, a baseball mitt and an old stocking hat met her eye. Curiously she moved them aside. A fishing rod, scrapbook, a small deer statue . . .

"Mickey!" Loretta's voice wafted in through the open window.

Quickly, Mickey pushed the curio aside and shut the closet door. At the window she turned, "Good-bye, aerie in the sky."

She descended hurriedly, first one branch, then another. And then . . .

"We wanted a younger child—one who was more,

you know—more moldable—and more feminine."

Mickey froze, hardly daring to breathe. She leaned forward, pushing a perfumed branch to one side. She saw the narrow dark band in Loretta's smooth dark hair and heard another voice murmur something unintelligible.

"She won't even let us call her Michelle but insists on Mickey!" Loretta exclaimed. The door closed softly behind her.

The heat rose in Mickey's face. Swiftly, she grasped the branch at her feet with her hands and swung, monkey-fashion, onto the ground.

She ran for the basement door, then stopped. Loretta and her unseen friend would probably be upstairs, and there would be no way to avoid them unless, unless . . .

She turned and scuttled around the house, creeping behind the garage. Her window was open. It only took a moment to wriggle in.

She stuffed a change of underwear, an extra shirt and jeans, and a comb into her brown duffel bag, then she was out the window and away.

The only road leading away from the house was steep and curved like a coiled snake. She left the road and headed for the brush, scrambling straight up the hillside. Her chest began to ache and her breath to come in short little gasps before she slowed to a limping climb.

"They don't want me," she whispered. "Not Kent, not Steve, not even Loretta!"

Hurt slithered up and wrapped itself around her throat. She tried to concentrate instead on the soft, steep slope, spongy with fir needles. Then the road was before her again.

She hesitated briefly, then leaped the ditch. Once across, she leaned against the rough bark of a straight, tall fir and looked back.

A bird winged high over her head, flying in the direction of the stream—her stream—or almost her stream. Through the trees she glimpsed the Middletons' pink house with the fish hatchery and its adjacent buildings stretched before it. The view made her think of the bottom of a great bowl, and she, high on its edge, looking down into it.

A sudden thought stabbed her. *I never got a chance to visit the hatchery.* And then, *I'll never see my aerie in the sky again, either. Oh, if only it had been the place . . .*

She shivered. The warmth of the afternoon sunshine was now gone. She turned, the hillside, thickly carpeted with ferns and wild strawberry plants, ascended before her. Dusky shadows lurked beneath the trees.

But Mickey went forward. The branches caught her short dark hair, moss clung to her sweater.

She stumbled again onto the graveled country road. A lone star winked at her. A winged creature swooped close to her head. An unidentified dark bulk loomed close. Brilliant headlights shone through the gloom, momentarily blinding her.

Mickey's fingers tightened on her duffel bag. She swallowed miserably. Loretta got out of the car and walked to the other side, opening the door.

"Get in, Mickey," Loretta said. "I've been waiting."

A part of Mickey wanted to whisper, "I'm sorry, Loretta," but the other part cried, "Why did you come after me? You don't really want me! Do you?"

Numbly she climbed into the car. "How did you know I was gone?" she asked.

"I wanted you to meet my friend, Lucille. When I couldn't find you, I went to your room. Your drawers were open—"

"Why—why did you come after me?" she whispered, struggling to keep her voice from breaking.

"Why do you think?" Loretta asked, slipping behind the wheel.

Mickey peered through the darkness, trying to see Loretta's face. She opened her mouth, but no words came.

"I came because I *care* about you," Loretta said slowly.

"Oh, no you don't!" Mickey cried. "I heard . . ."

"What is it you think you heard?"

"You said you wanted someone younger! Someone more—more girlish—"

Loretta's arm suddenly slid around Mickey's shoulders. "You didn't hear the rest, did you?"

"I—I—"

"I told Lucille that *that* was what I had in my mind. But as soon as I saw you, I knew you were the one I wanted to take into my home—my heart."

"But!"

"I know. Try to understand, Mickey. What people have in their mind isn't necessarily what they really want! As soon as I saw your big dark eyes, that fly-away soft, dark hair, I knew—"

"But Kent!"

Loretta's arm tightened around her. "Kent has his own private hell to deal with. And I—Please, Mickey, won't you give us a chance?"

Mickey turned toward her in the darkness, a funny warm feeling rising inside her. Was it true? Did Loretta really care about her?

She did come after me, Mickey reasoned. If she didn't care, she wouldn't have, would she? Mickey leaned back in the seat, her thoughts a jumble of too many new feelings, new impressions.

Together they drove back down the curvy, windy road. Back to the stream—and—Mickey drew in her breath sharply—Joel?

Three / At the Fish Hatchery

Mickey wakened the next morning to the smell of frying bacon. She sniffed appreciatively and bounced out of bed.

She stepped into blue cords while she debated whether to wear the plaid shirt, the red-and-white checked blouse or the long-sleeved, dark-blue pullover.

She decided on the blue pullover and pulled it on, critically examining her reflection in the mirror—tousled dark hair, eyes that looked too big for her small, heart-shaped face, lips slightly parted, needing a touch of color.

Kent's unexpected roar, "Breakfast! Come and get it!" galvanized her to action. Her comb whisked through her hair before another shout propelled her through the door.

Kent stood in front of the kitchen stove, legs braced apart, brandishing a turner. He grinned at her, yesterday's animosity apparently forgotten.

"Sit down," he invited. "I'll dish you up."

He thrust in front of her a plate piled high with

steaming scrambled eggs and crisp bacon. Steve slid into the chair opposite her and lifted his brows. A long, slow wink closed one eye.

An unexpected sense of belonging enwrapped Mickey. She grinned back at him.

"It's Saturday," Steve said. "Want to tour the fish hatchery with me?"

"Do they let you do that?" Mickey asked.

"Sure do." He took a big bite of his eggs. "A lot of the guys who work there are my friends now. I go over there a lot."

"It sounds interesting," Mickey said tentatively. "Can we go inside the buildings?"

"They take people through all the time," Loretta said from the doorway.

She sat down beside Mickey and smiled at her husband. She looked fresh, young and girlish, dressed in a crisp striped blouse and dark slacks. "Where's my breakfast?" she called.

"Adam and Eve on a raft and wreck'um!" Kent called back. He plopped Loretta's eggs onto a piece of toast and carried her plate with exaggerated courtesy to the table.

Mickey turned away as he bent to kiss Loretta. But Loretta was unembarrassed.

"So, it's the fish hatchery for you, is it?" she asked.

Steve stood up with a mumbled, "Excuse me, meet you out front," and vanished out the door.

Kent scowled after him. "I wish he wouldn't do that eat and run business."

But Loretta was unperturbed. "He'll grow up fast enough. Kids do you know—"

Kent pushed back his chair. "Steve!" he roared. Bits of his angry lecture drifted in through the open door. "Ungrateful—discourteous—thinking only of yourself."

Loretta got up and began to clear the table.

"Let me," Mickey volunteered.

"No, thanks. Go on now. You can help with dinner things instead."

Steve was sitting on the front steps, his shoulders bowed, his arms clasping his knees. He looked up as Mickey opened the door. "Ready?"

"Sure!"

They hurried across the lawn and out the front gate. "Ever been to a fish hatchery?" Steve wanted to know.

Mickey shook her head.

"There really isn't much to see. But it is sort of interesting—if you like that sort of thing." He lifted his head. "What do you like to do?"

"Why, I—I—"

His eyes widened in amazement. "You mean you don't know?" he asked incredulously.

"Well, I like to read—" Mickey floundered. "And sometimes I think I might like to learn to cook."

She fell silent, her thoughts a jumble of confusion. What did she like anyway? Skating?—a little, but not much, not since she'd fallen and the awful boy with the freckles had teased her unrelentingly.

Pictures of her foster homes flickered through her mind. She remembered camping with the Alexanders, learning to crochet from Mom Appleby. But most of all, she remembered the running, the awful feeling of not really belonging, of searching for something—she wasn't sure what. And then, when the restless feeling got too bad—she'd just take off—

"I'm sorry, Mickey," Mrs. Morton, her caseworker had explained. "There isn't any way we're going to keep you out of juvenile home if you keep running off."

Then Loretta had come . . .

"Well," Steve interrupted. "What else?"

"What else what?"

"What else do you like to do?" he repeated.

"I don't know." Mickey's thoughts twisted. "What about you? What do you like?"

Steve picked up a rock and tossed it in the air. "Lots of things," he said airily, "like swimming, fishing, comics. I even like school."

"I don't," Mickey said flatly.

"That's stupid. You have to go, so you might as well like it."

Her fear of new schools, new faces, rose inside her. Would she always be on the fringes—never quite belonging?

"School hasn't been much fun for me," she muttered. "I've been in lots of them and I've never, ever seemed to fit."

She searched for words to explain the paralyzing fear that gripped her every time she stepped onto a new campus. But no words came.

She stamped her foot instead, rattling the road rocks. "I'm not going back."

"I bet Dad and Mom say you do," Steve countered.

Mickey shrugged. "Maybe I'll just leave. And this time I'll find a way to disappear—" But even as she said it, she wondered. There was something about the Middletons. Her wish to be their girl intensified each day she was with them.

"We're here," Steve exclaimed. He pointed to a large cement pond encircled by a metal mesh fence. "This is the adult holding tank."

Mickey stopped at the edge, her fingers clawing the thick wires. She peered into the water. "I can't see anything—oh, yes, I can! They're big aren't they?"

"Come on over here," Steve called. He stood beside the waist-high concrete runways, motioning to her. "This is the spawning channel."

Mickey followed and stood beside him. "I can see them better here," she observed.

Steve hurried on to another runway. "This is where they keep the smaller ones."

Mickey ran over to him. "Oh," she murmured, "the little darlings." She felt a great urge to lean over the edge and let the silver fish swim between her fingers.

"Look there," Steve gestured toward a young man walking briskly on the steel grate walkway between the holding tanks. With simple rhythm he dipped his hand into the bucket, then tossed fish food over the water. The water dimpled with movement. Then dip, toss, dip, toss and more sparkling dimples.

He quit tossing as he came up to them, his quick glance darting questioningly over to Mickey. He extended the bucket toward her. "Would you like to feed the fish?"

Mickey drew in a quick excited breath. "Please." She pulled out a handful of coarse fish food and tossed it into the tank that held the baby silver. Immediately the water bubbled with action.

"They're so fast," Mickey marveled, "and so little. I can hardly believe it!"

"Mickey, this is my friend, Jim." Steve explained.

"Jim, this is Mickey, my new sister."

Reluctantly, Mickey tore her attention from the water and looked at the man beside them. Faded blue jeans and a brown khaki shirt made him look a part of the gray cement and the brownish water. But the blue eyes that contrasted so neatly with his dark beard and hair brimmed with questions. The line between his brows deepened.

"Your new sister?"

"Yep," Steve explained. "She's only been here five days, so she's really new—even if she is three years older than I am!"

A wistful sadness crinkled around Jim's eyes. His nose twitched suddenly. He glanced down, almost shyly. *Like a rabbit,* Mickey thought.

There was an awkward pause. She gestured nervously toward the pink house. "I'm living there now," she said.

Jim looked up. "So you're the new daughter of the house," he mused. Something in the tone of his voice made sadness well up in Mickey. She didn't know what to say.

She was glad Steve came to her rescue. "I'd like to show Mickey where you keep the newly hatched babies. She's never been inside a hatchery before."

Jim nodded slowly. Once again, Mickey was sure she saw his nose twitch. Then he smiled and the rabbit illusion disappeared.

"I'll take you through as soon as I finish feeding. Okay if I meet you in the lounge in about ten minutes?"

Mickey and Steve nodded. "We'll look around outside first," Steve said.

Jim tossed another handful of food over the water. Once again the magical ripples dipped and swirled. Mickey watched the dimples follow him.

What a strange man he was, she marveled. *So sad and wistful, and the intent way he'd looked at her! Had she reminded him of someone he'd seen before—someone who might have brought him pain?*

She found herself wishing she could learn more about him. It surprised her a little. She didn't often think about other people and their troubles.

"He's different," she said, "different—but nice."

Steve stared at her. "Now don't start going all girl and getting goo-gaw over him!"

"I'm not!" Mickey cried indignantly. She giggled suddenly. "How old is he anyway?"

Steve shrugged. "He must be close to thirty. He's been to college, and he told me once that it took him extra time because he worked his way through."

"College! To feed fish?"

Steve gave her a withering look. "For goodness sakes, that isn't all he does! He majored in fishery. That takes five years! And I happen to know he has a girlfriend in California. He told me about her once."

Mickey tossed her head. "Well, they must not be much in love! If it were me, he wouldn't be up here in Oregon and me down there in California, that's for sure!"

"For crying out loud! You must be getting sweet on him!"

A ripple of laughter bubbled to Mickey's lips. "Of course I'm not! I was just thinking that if I were in love, I'd stick close! Peter Rabbit isn't my type, but someday there might be somebody who is."

"Peter Rabbit! Who's Peter Rabbit?"

"Oh," Mickey said loftily, "your friend, Jim. The way he twitches his nose and sort of lowers his eyes."

A startled awareness leaped into Steve's eyes. "You know," he said thoughtfully, "he does, doesn't he?"

"And I don't mean it badly, either. It's just that people remind me of animals sometimes. I went to school once with a girl who reminded me of a little field mouse."

"What do I remind you of?"

"I don't know. It doesn't always come. But I think your father is rather like a lion. He roars—and growls, too."

"And courage, he has courage."

"I wouldn't know about that. But come on. I want to look at that tank over there."

"They're called runways," Steve corrected.

Mickey nodded. "The fish must be segregated according to size," she noted, "then put in different tanks—runways, I mean."

At the hatchery entrance, Jim opened the door. They went at once to a big, cool room where the outer walls were stacked with gray trays.

Jim gestured toward the trays. "The eggs are kept there."

Mickey peered inside a tray. "They look like soft boiled beads," she said, shuddering. She turned to the long, green runways, in the middle of the room. "This is more interesting."

It was a fascinating world she peered into. Minute babies swam in their own protected world, apart from natural predators.

Even Jim seemed different inside these walls. His shyness vanished as he spoke with quiet assurance.

"We've been doing something comparatively new here this year. We've discovered that when we raise the water temperature slightly during the winter months, it speeds their growth."

Mickey touched the water with an exploring finger. The tiny fish scattered like droplets of water. "Do many of them die?"

"Not really. We do have to fight a kidney disease that takes some of the older ones." He shook his head. "A fish has a million enemies, but the worst of all is man. For example, poaching is a big problem in this creek."

Steve gave an excited jump. "Every day, all summer, when the creek is closed to anglers, the state police park, get out and walk along the bank."

Jim nodded. "We owe our state police a lot of thanks. It's impossible for the hatchery personnel to protect the stream—alone. And poaching isn't the only problem."

"Pollution?" Mickey asked.

"Yes. Keeping the stream well stocked is our number one job, but keeping the stream clean is everybody's job. We need more people to be aware of what pollutes a stream and reduces our fish population."

On the way back to the house, Steve and Mickey talked about it.

"It almost makes you want to be involved," Mickey explained.

"I already am," Steve said wisely. "That's what I'll be studying in college."

"College!" Mickey exclaimed. "But you're not even in high school!"

Steve shrugged. "Doesn't matter. High school offers a lot—biology—chemistry—" He raised his eyebrows at her. "It helps to know where you're going."

A sudden shame welled up inside her as she stared at Steve, a thin stick of a boy with pale, blue-gray eyes, not really very sure of himself. His words rolled guiltily in her mind.

Here she was, three years older, and all she thought about was running away, and—boys.

She looked past Steve and saw someone coming toward them, bright head held high, a fishing pole in hand.

Mickey's heart did a heavy clump. Joel. What would she say to him—or he to her? Or would he say nothing because Kent had yelled at him? Mickey stopped and waited.

Four / Margot

But it wasn't Joel. Instead it was a girl who looked amazingly like him.

She had his bright hair, the same lifting of the chin, the long body. Even her shoulders were broad and moved with simple grace in response to her long strides.

Mickey stared. She walked easily, as though she was accustomed to rough country roads. How poised she was, how elegant!

Then the girl smiled, her kind lips tinted with soft pink. Her smile deepened. Mickey forgot her apprehension.

"You must be Mickey. Joel asked me to come and see firsthand if you were okay. No pneumonia, huh?"

Mickey shook her head. Then the girl smiled at Steve, who awkwardly ground the toe of his shoe into the road.

"How does it feel to have a sister?"

"It's okay," Steve muttered. He sidled toward the edge of the road, obviously anxious to get on with his own affairs.

Quickly Mickey came to his rescue. "Thanks a lot for showing me around the hatchery, Steve. Maybe I can return the favor."

Steve nodded and shot off like over-warm Coke popping from its bottle.

"He's at the age where he doesn't like girls, isn't he?" The girl who looked so much like Joel smiled approvingly at Mickey. "He acted like he likes you though."

"I think he does—a little." Mickey didn't explain that it was only since her mishap in the creek that he'd begun to warm to her. Instead she said, "You must be Joel's older sister."

"No—younger—by a year. I'm Tam—for Tamera. I hope we can be friends, Mickey." She gestured with a long graceful hand. "I could never have too many."

Me either, Mickey wanted to say. But she didn't. Friends had been in short supply for her. She looked at Tam speculatively. Would this long-legged, sure creature be the hazy outline she'd visualized in the upstairs room?

Well, why not? She *was* Joel's sister, wasn't she? And Joel was, well—already she sensed he was somebody special.

She had a sudden longing to take Tam up the steep stairs into her aerie. If only Loretta . . .

She turned to Tam shyly. "Would you like to come home with me? Loretta fixed me a room."

"Love it," Tam smiled. "Is your room pink like the outside of the house?" she asked curiously.

Mickey stopped, startled. "How did you know?"

"I didn't." Tam laughed and took Mickey's arm. "I was only guessing. Let's run!"

Both girls were breathless when Mickey opened the

door of her room. "Why, it's lovely," Tam exclaimed. She collapsed on the bed and looked around. "But it doesn't look much like you, does it?"

"No—o. Not at all."

Tam locked both hands behind her head, tilting it thoughtfully to one side. "Rooms should, you know, look like their owners. But of course, Loretta didn't know you when she decorated, did she?"

Mickey shook her head. "What do you think would suit me?"

"I'm not exactly sure. I don't know you very well yet. But I don't think you're the fluttering feminine type. This room needs someone who's a little bit fragile, maybe—"

Mickey leaned forward. "Would wooden paneling and Indian blankets and rag rugs suit me better?"

Tam smiled. "Is that what you like?"

"Yes. And lots of windows to let the outside in. This room is so closed up it gives me the willies." She gestured toward the curtained window. "All you can see is the backside of the garage."

"Maybe you can change it. New curtains or something. Or would that hurt Loretta's feelings?"

"I'm not sure. I might ask."

They chatted on, content to get acquainted, for some time. Tam sat up, glancing at her watch. "I should leave now. Mickey, I'm coming again, if it's all right."

"All right!" Mickey exclaimed. "It would be wonderful. I don't know anybody around here at all."

"Well, you know me now," Tam said. She got up, stretching like a lazy cat.

After she left, Mickey hugged Tam's words to herself. *She acts like she likes me,* she marveled. *She really does. Oh, if only I could have the room upstairs.*

On impulse Mickey went in search of Loretta. She found her downstairs sorting the contents of the hall closet.

Loretta held up a blue denim jacket, obviously too small for anyone in the family. "Why do people keep such things?" she wondered aloud.

"Loretta—" Mickey said uncertainly.

Loretta put the jacket down and looked at her. "What is it, Mickey?"

Mickey licked her lips. "It's about my room—"

"What about it?"

"I—I don't know—exactly. It just doesn't seem to fit."

"Fit?"

"Fit me." Mickey searched for words. "It's all very lovely, too lovely for me. I'm not like that."

Loretta ran her fingers through her dark hair. "I don't think I understand, Mickey."

"It isn't easy to explain," Mickey said. "It's not that I don't appreciate its being so beautiful and all—It just isn't me!"

"What is you, then?"

"Something plain and open! My room is closed up—like—like a coffin!" She stopped as a pained look crossed Loretta's face. "I'm sorry," she whispered. "I didn't mean to be ungrateful."

"It's all right, Mickey," Loretta said softly. She looked at the clothes piled on the floor without seeming to see them. "Let's go upstairs. We need to talk."

The tightness of a vise gripped Mickey's throat as she

followed Loretta up the stairs and into the pink room. Sudden tears blurred her eyes. She hadn't meant to hurt Loretta!

Loretta pulled the white wicker chair close as Mickey sank onto the bed. "There's something I need to tell you, Mickey. It's painful, and I never thought I'd need to bring it up again. But—

"This room belonged to Margot, my stepdaughter." A faraway look veiled Loretta's eyes. "She was a lovely girl, much like you, Mickey, with dark hair and eyes. No, I know what you're thinking—she wasn't fragile and feminine. That was only *my* dream. She was something else—strong-willed, vibrant, popular with the boys, even though she was only 15.

"I let her go swimming that day against my better judgment. She told me she was meeting her girlfriend and that they were going to the whale rock up the creek. I never dreamed she would go alone.

"Her brother, Jami, was in the woods when she cried for help. He came quickly, but he panicked—"

"Loretta! You don't have to tell me—"

Loretta lifted her head. "Yes, I do, Mickey. You've come into an unhappy family, and it's only right you know. And you're so like her—but so different—

"We lost Jami that day, too. His father blamed him for not jumping in after Margot. Perhaps if he had, he could have saved her. We'll never know. He ran for help instead."

"What happened to him?"

"Kent went into one of his black rages. Jami was barely 18, but Kent couldn't control his grief. He lashed at Jami horribly.

"I think Kent was ashamed of him. Jami was so different from his father. Quiet, gentle, unsure of himself. He had those drifting hands that don't take hold—"

Loretta gestured with her own, a helpless gesture that twisted in Mickey's heart. "We never saw Jami again. I think Kent hurt him too much. And Kent wouldn't go after him. So there we were, left alone, Kent and I and our four-year-old Steve.

"I wanted to make it up to Kent by having a daughter to take Margot's place, but it never happened. I was depressed for months. Kent's two children—and mine too—both gone."

Mickey blinked hard. "Is that why you wanted me?"

"In a way, maybe. But it's been nine years now, Mickey. One can't go back. Not really."

Loretta stood up and walked to the dressing table. She fingered the pink tulle. "This room hasn't been used much since Margot died. Most of the time it's been closed and we tried to forget . . ."

"But what made you—"

Loretta turned, her smile gentle. "I needed a girl," she said simply. "When I saw you, I knew you were the one. Now about this room. What would you like to do? Fresh paint, wallpaper, new curtains?"

Mickey took a long deep breath. "Do you think I could make it look a little like the room at the top of the stairs? The Indian blanket—"

Loretta's fingers suddenly clenched the fragile pink material, her knuckles showing white. "You were up there?" she asked. "Why, Kent—Kent—"

"I climbed up the tree and went in the window," Mickey confessed. "I'm sorry."

"Just don't tell Kent! He gave strict orders that the room was to be forgotten when Jami left!"

Mickey stared at her uncomprehendingly. "But why?"

"I think it was because deep down he thought Jami would change—come home someday—"

"Then I won't be able—"

"No, Mickey. You know Kent—or do you? He gets one idea in his head, and he never gives up."

A shiver ran up Mickey's arms; she remembered a shouting, angry man glowering in rage, standing on the creek bank. *But he was hurting,* she thought with sudden understanding. *He was seeing his Margot—under the water.*

"But you can repaint this room," Loretta said. "I'll talk to Kent about it." She turned at the door, smiling. "Start planning your colors."

Mickey leaned back, pushing the pillow into a bigger lump under her head. But she wasn't thinking about colors. She was thinking about Loretta. Once more her eyes examined the room's details. She also saw an uncertain young stepmother planning ruffled curtains, selecting dainty pink material and fragile ribbons.

And she saw something else. She saw two hurting parents who had in one day lost two children. Mickey shivered and turned onto her stomach, burying her face in the pillow.

That afternoon clouds built up, obscuring the pale spring sunshine. Mickey slipped into a jacket and hurried outdoors, eager to get better acquainted with the creek before the rain began.

She sped across the lawn as Steve came in the gate.

"Hi!" she called. "Where've you been?"

He grinned as he latched the gate. "Talking to Jim. I even got to help him a little while—"

The door to the house opened and Kent came toward them. There was a dark thundering look on his face, and Mickey caught her breath. Had she somehow made him angry?

"Steve!" Kent roared. "Where have you been?"

Steve dropped his chin. The tip of his shoe started moving against the cement walk. "At—at the hatchery. I was helping—"

Kent tossed him a withering look. "What do you mean helping? You were supposed to be cleaning out the garage! I told you earlier—and off you went!" He slammed his fist into his palm. "When I give you a job I expect you to do it! How do you ever expect to amount to anything if you don't learn responsibility?"

"I was going to! But I thought—"

"The trouble is you don't think!"

But Steve was already scuttling to the garage. A lump swelled up inside Mickey's throat. Why couldn't Kent see the light that shone from Steve's eyes when he talked about the hatchery—about Jim?

She opened her lips for an angry retort, then clamped them shut. This was no time to get between a father and his son.

By evening the rain had begun. All night it lashed the window, driven by a wind that moaned through the fir trees.

Once Mickey wakened to the far-off sound of voices in the darkness—arguing voices, pained voices. *Kent,* she thought, *Loretta.* Then, *Margot—Jami—*

Mickey shoved her head beneath the pillow and tried to go back to sleep. The wind and rain, instead of lulling her, roused unhappy memories.

She saw her long-ago self: a small girl with blazing eyes shouting at another child.

"Don't call me Michelle! I'm Mickey! Only my mama calls me Michelle!"

And then the awful hurt—her mother gone—

Her mother's face, almost forgotten, floated in un-bidden, her long dark hair blowing in the wind. Mickey had last seen her driving off in a battered station wagon, her two brothers tucked in front, the back loaded with suitcases and boxes.

Then descending darkness—her mother was gone—really gone.

Then a new face floated toward her—Margot, her pensive face long but strikingly attractive, her dark eyes sparkling with mischief and dare-deviltry.

Resolutely Mickey pushed it aside, but Margot returned, her eyes teasing. "Come on!" she shouted, and she shoved Mickey beneath the cold water of the rushing stream—

Mickey jerked awake, drenched in cold sweat, wondering how long she'd been asleep. She looked at the clock—4:30.

Determinedly she shoved the faces aside and thought of a huge, white cherry tree that grew and grew until she was lost in its branches . . .

When she wakened, the house was quiet. She felt a sudden urgency to see the cherry tree, to touch its blossoms.

She jumped out of bed, grabbing her dark brown corduroy robe. Barefoot, she slipped down the stairs and out of the basement entrance.

The great white tree lowered its wet, sweet-scented branches toward her. Gently, Mickey pulled one close to her nose.

The quiet squeak of a hinge made her turn. Kent Middleton stood in the doorway, his legs braced apart, his arms folded. He cleared his throat uneasily.

"Loretta said you'd like to move into the room upstairs," he said. "You may do it whenever you wish."

The cherry branch jerked upward as Mickey flew toward him. "Oh, sir," she cried. "Thank you. Thank you."

Then Kent's arms were around her. He awkwardly patted her shoulder. "Now, now. You just run on back and start moving your things. I've already unlocked the door."

Breathlessly Mickey disengaged herself. "Oh, Mr. Middleton—"

"You can call me Kent," he said. "And if that doesn't suit, Uncle Kent will do." He turned and walked toward the stream, a lonely figure with shoulders squared and rigid.

"Uncle Kent," Mickey murmured. "My very own Uncle Kent." Then she was racing up the stairs two steps at a time.

"Loretta," she cried. "I get to move upstairs, right now—today!"

The iron skillet in Loretta's hand clattered onto the stove. "Why, Mickey," she cried, "did Kent really—"

Mickey clasped her hands together and nodded. "He

told me just now! I can move in right away! I really can. And he said I could call him Uncle Kent."

To Mickey's amazement, Loretta covered her face with her hands.

"Loretta?" Mickey whispered uncertainly. "I—if you'd rather I didn't—"

"It isn't what you think, dear girl." She lowered her hands and smiled tremulously. "There's nothing I'd like better than to have that room used. It's been like a tomb—a silent reminder—"

She put her hand on Mickey's shoulder. "To think—" she marveled, "he asked you to call him Uncle Kent. Perhaps—after nine years—some healing has begun."

Five / The Spirit of the Stream

Mickey and Loretta stood in the middle of the aerie and looked around.

"It's going to need a thorough cleaning with plenty of soap and water," Loretta exclaimed, wrinkling her nose. "But first let's empty the closet."

Memories of a tiny wooden deer and an old scrapbook urged Mickey to step forward. "Let me," she volunteered. "I'll put everything in a box, and you can go through it later—"

Loretta nodded and walked to the window. Rain pounded against it. She drew her finger across the glass. "You'll need window cleaner—" Her gaze drifted to the desk, "and furniture polish—rags—"

"I can do everything," Mickey said eagerly.

Loretta smiled. "Of course." She moved to the bed. "I'll bring up fresh sheets—more blankets." She pulled on the edge of the bright Indian blanket. "Like this, huh?"

"Love it!" Mickey exclaimed. She felt a sudden desire for Loretta to be gone, so she might taste alone the joy of possession. "Could I start right away?"

Loretta wandered around the room, lightly touching furniture and decorations. She leaned against the window frame and looked out through the rain sluicing against the windowpane.

"The creek is on the rise," she said. "If this rain keeps on the steelhead will move upstream."

"Why?" Mickey wondered.

"They like the high water. Fishermen lie awake praying for it." Loretta turned from the window.

Please go, Mickey pleaded silently. *Go now.*

With a last look around, Loretta reached for the doorknob. "I'll get what you need, Mickey. There're boxes in the garage—"

Impulsively, Mickey covered Loretta's hand with her own. "Thank you."

Loretta shrugged. "I thank *you*, Mickey. And somehow I think Jami would thank you, too. This room needed to be used—not kept locked like a mausoleum."

"What about Margot's?"

"We've never kept it locked. Guests use it sometimes. I'd like to redecorate it maybe. But its such an impossible room, and I had no heart for it." Loretta sighed deeply. "If you have any ideas . . ."

After Loretta left, Mickey opened the closet. The leftover reminders of a lost boyhood peered at her; a battered baseball mitt, a bat propped in the corner, the old scrapbook.

"Steve might like these," Mickey murmured, pulling them onto the floor. She reached for the carved deer, turning it in her hands.

It's lovely, she thought, *so fragile—so real.* Her fingers caressed its pricked ears, the graceful neck. Thoughtfully, she put it with the mitt and bat. A bag of marbles followed. Then another small wooden carving. This one was a fox, its head bent low, as if scuttling through the brush, away from an enemy.

I wonder if Jami carved these, Mickey mused. *But they're so perfect.* She put the fox beside the deer and pushed her hand to the back of the shelf. Her fingertips brushed something large and ungainly.

A totem pole, about two feet tall and exquisitely carved, rolled into her hands. Mickey's wondering fingers traced the figure of a beaver—a deer. At the top, a large eagle had been freed from the wood. Its fierce eyes glared at her; its wings spread wide, threatening, yet somehow protecting.

"The spirit of the creek," Mickey muttered involuntarily.

Excitement leaped in her as she examined the base. There was a slim trout, a crayfish, a nymph . . .

"Oh!" she cried as she discerned a water skipper astride the clearly defined water surface. Then, "a dragon fly! Its tail is in the water! It must be laying eggs. And there's a fallen leaf—"

She turned the pole in her hands, marveling at the uniqueness of its workmanship.

After a while, she set it beside the bat and stepped back. "You don't belong there," she said. "You should be sitting on a rock high above the creek."

Suddenly she wanted to share her find with Loretta. As she hurried down the stairs, her feet seemed to stop of their own accord. Doubts flashed in her mind. *Was this the right thing to do?*

Loretta had had too much hurt, she decided. She would pack the totem pole into a box with the rest of Jami's things and say nothing.

But she didn't. The pole looked out of place and forlorn, sitting awkwardly among cast-off sweaters and forgotten rackets.

Before she took the box downstairs, Mickey lifted out the totem pole and put it back into the closet. She hesitated briefly, then put the fox and deer beside it. The old scrapbook followed. Later she would decide what to do with them.

Mickey spent the remainder of the day cleaning. The rain slacked off a bit toward evening, and she was amazed to see a dozen or more fishermen converge on the stream. She leaned out her window, eager to see if Joel might be among them. But there was no sight of curly, reddish-brown hair, nor shoulders that moved with his peculiar grace.

Mickey wakened the next morning to a whirl of activity. The kitchen table was cluttered with cornflakes, toast crumbs, and sticky strawberry jam knives. Kent had already gone, and Loretta stood by the stove buttering her toast.

"You'll have to fix something yourself," she said. "It's my morning to work at the pharmacy." She gestured toward the sink. "If you could put the potatoes into the oven at four-thirty and make a salad, I'd appreciate it. I can do the rest when I get home." She went out the kitchen door, her toast still clutched in her hand.

"It's always like this the day Mom works," Steve grumbled from the door. "Yuck!"

He too disappeared. He came back a few minutes later lugging a pile of books and flopped them on the table.

He eyed her curiously. "Think you can stand it all by yourself for a whole day?" he asked.

Mickey shrugged. She almost wished she'd waited to move into her new room. But it was too late for that. Her first night in her aerie was behind her, a night of tossing firs and rain, the roar of the stream. She peered out the kitchen window.

"Won't this rain ruin the cherry blossoms?" she asked. But Steve was running out to catch a ride up the hill with an obliging neighbor.

The day dragged worse than Mickey dreamed it would. After she had cleaned the kitchen, scrubbed the potatoes and planned the salad, there was nothing else to do.

Or was there? The creek outside roared an invitation. Mickey shrugged into a hooded sweatshirt and hurried to meet it. Swollen with the rains, darkened with run-off, it no longer sang sweetly.

But Mickey didn't care. A strange excitement filled her as she faced the wind and felt the spray wet her face. She went across the bridge below the hatchery and down the other side of the creek. Mossy vine maples mingled with drooping cedars. Tall sword ferns brushed her jeans.

The stream fascinated her. It roared and raced over huge rocks. Like a mighty giant, it pushed an occasional limb along and drew small sticks into its current, propelling them downstream.

Mickey went around the bend, parting the bushes

ahead of her. There stood Joel on a log jutting into the stream. He turned.

"Mickey!' he exclaimed. He balanced carefully, then ran lightly toward her.

"I thought you were in school," Mickey blurted uncertainly.

"Got out at noon. Teacher's workday." He looked at her intently. "What're you up to?"

"The creek," she explained. "It looks so different."

Joel nodded. "It's in its wild mood now. I love it." He grinned. "It's sort of exciting, isn't it?"

"Yes, it is." She changed the subject. "I looked for you yesterday. I thought you might be fishing—many were out."

Joel shook his head. "Sunday is a family day at our house. We go to church in the morning—and in the evening."

"Really?" Mickey looked at him with open curiosity. "Why?"

"Why?" Joel's green eyes regarded her steadily. "Because Jesus Christ is an important part of my life—" He hesitated. "Actually, He's my entire life."

"Your entire life?" Mickey exclaimed. She picked up a stick and tossed it into the swirling current. "I've never been inside a church in my life—and Jesus Christ— well—I never even think of Him."

"Want to come to church with me?" Joel asked.

Mickey squatted on the ground, resting her elbows on her knees, carefully balancing on her toes. "I don't know," she said. She looked up. "What do you do there?"

"We study the Bible in our Sunday school class,

sing—then listen to what our pastor has to say from God's Word. It's neat."

"Neat?"

Joel got down beside her, his fingers busy peeling a small twig. "Church is special to me, Mickey. It's my family. And that's where Jesus Christ comes into it. He's our God, our Lord, and we love Him. It makes us eager to get together. Didn't any of your foster parents, or your real mom and dad take you?"

Mickey shook her head. "Mom Appleby used to go. But she always said she wouldn't force religion down anybody's throat. So I never went."

She leaped to her feet. "Someday maybe I will. But not right now. Look, Joel. There—up the creek—it looks like an animal."

Joel's eyes followed the direction of her pointing finger. "Let's go!" he exclaimed. He began to run. Mickey followed, over rocks, across jutting roots. As she came nearer she realized it was a young doe, caught in the swirling creek.

"Oh, the poor thing," she cried, "will she die?"

Joel didn't answer. The deer struggled helplessly. Mickey could clearly see the fear in her dark, liquid eyes. The deer reminded her of the carving high on her closet shelf. She caught her breath.

"I'm going in after her!" Joel exclaimed.

He plunged into the water and waded into the middle of the stream. As he drew close, Mickey saw dark fear flare in the deer's eyes.

"Oh, beautiful lady," Mickey whispered. "You are the spirit of the creek. Don't be afraid . . ."

Joel reached the deer. Both hands touched her neck

then went beneath the water.

"She's caught on a log," he shouted. "I can't budge her—"

"I'll come," Mickey called. The icy water splashed around her ankles, and she shuddered.

"Wait—" Joel cried, "go for help—"

But Mickey kept on. The water rose high on her legs, then to her waist. Her foot caught on a rock, and she staggered forward, gasping as the water rose nearly chest deep. Joel's hand reached out to her, and for an instant she clung tightly. Then she was beside him.

"If you could push down the limb while I shove on her rear, I think we can get her free."

Mickey obeyed. The limb was deep and she was wet to her neck, but she didn't care. The lovely doe's face was close to her own.

"Don't be afraid," she whispered; "we're here to help." Was that a flicker of trust?

She gulped a mouthful of water, then shoved hard on the branch, suddenly conscious of Joel's hand touching hers. The deer moved. Mickey lurched backwards. She clutched the submerged log, catching herself.

Joel's face was close to hers. "All right?"

Mickey nodded. She put her arms around the deer's neck and began to pull her toward the shore. Joel pushed on her withers, speaking encouraging words. The little deer's hooves struck the rocks. Together they lifted her onto the shore.

The doe's legs couldn't hold her. She took one step forward and collapsed.

Joel and Mickey looked at each other.

"Call the hatchery," Joel gasped, pushing his soaked

hair off his forehead.

Mickey nodded numbly, turned and ran. Her clothes clung to her, hampering her stride.

Moments later she burst through the basement door, muddy footsteps trailing her up the stairs and into the spotless kitchen. Her trembling fingers raced down the numbers, then fumbled with the dial.

"We just pulled a deer out of the creek—" she explained through chattering teeth. "Its alive—"

"And who is we?" a courteous male voice asked.

"We're the pink house just below you. We—"

"I'll send the manager right away. Wait there."

Mickey put the receiver down, her thoughts tumbling. *First, change clothes, second, find one of Kent's jackets for Joel, third, maybe a blanket to cover the deer.* She rushed up the stairs.

She flopped her clothes into a soaking heap on her bedroom floor. She dressed quickly, then pulled her blanket from the bed. As she hurried downstairs, she grabbed a denim jacket from the hall closet.

She was out the door in time to meet Jim. He stood there awkwardly, ill at ease, worry lines radiating from his dark blue eyes. "You're—you're the manager?" Mickey asked, unable to hide the amazement in her voice.

"No—they sent me. The manager's off the grounds." A sudden smile relieved the frown lines on his forehead. "Now where is this swimming deer of yours?"

"Down the creek. Come on."

Without words the two followed the rushing stream to Joel and the trembling doe lying on the bank. Mickey tossed Joel the jacket, then bent over the deer.

"You poor, dear," she murmured. Gently, she spread her bright Indian blanket over the wet, dark brown form. "Will she live?"

Joel slipped on the jacket. "Not if we leave her here."

Jim nodded. The frown with which he'd met her at the door deepened as his fingers traced the bold gold and black design.

He looked up, his eyes intent on Mickey. "If we move her clear up to the hatchery, it'll be hard on her. Would your folks care if we took her inside to your basement—where it's warm?"

"Oh, sure," Mickey cried. "She'd be warm there."

Joel scowled. "Kent might be angry," he said, looking at Mickey.

Courage welled up inside Mickey as she looked at the frightened deer. "Kent and Loretta won't mind— I'm sure. And I could call them."

"They aren't there?" Jim asked, something like relief flitting across his face.

Mickey shook her head. "I'm home alone. But I'll accept the responsibility. Please—take her to our basement."

With quick decision, Jim bent and scooped up the deer, Indian blanket and all.

Joel and Mickey exchanged a look. Then, suddenly, Joel's hand was clasping Mickey's. They fell into step behind Jim.

Six / Deer in the Kitchen

"Best stand back a bit," Jim advised, "she's a wild creature." Gently he laid the doe on the basement floor.

Mickey stepped back, her eyes riveted on the beautiful animal. "Will—will she live?"

"She's got a good chance. But she's cold, clear through. She needs to warm up." He nodded toward Joel. "So does he."

"Oh," Mickey exclaimed. She tore her fascinated gaze from the doe and looked at Joel, touseled hair covering his brows. His jeans clung to him; his jacket showed wet streaks.

He shuddered, grinning through faintly blue lips. "Maybe I could borrow something of Kent's—"

Mickey dashed up the stairs. How thoughtless of his comfort she'd been, while for herself . . .

Feeling a ridiculous combination of intruder and shamed child, Mickey hurried into Kent and Loretta's bedroom. A girl in a picture frame on the walnut dresser dimpled at her. "Margot!" But this girl's face wasn't the

60

long pensive face of her dream. She sparkled a dimple, and her slightly parted lips had a beckoning, inviting, come-be-with-me look.

Trying not to think, Mickey began pulling out blue jeans, sweater, underwear and socks, then returned to the basement.

The color rose into her cheeks as she handed them to Joel. But he took them without comment, stepping into the adjoining bathroom.

Once again Mickey looked at the doe. A joyous exhilaration rose inside her as she saw those wild dark eyes, this time clear and unafraid, looking back at her.

Jim looked up. "May I leave her here with you?" he asked.

Mickey nodded. Reluctantly she regarded the man kneeling beside the doe. The strange wistfulness she'd noticed when she'd first met him at the hatchery was lurking in his eyes again. He bent down, smoothing the corner of the blanket.

How beautiful his hands are, Mickey marveled suddenly. *Could he be an artist, or a pianist?*

"If anything comes up you can call." Jim rose to his feet. "The most important thing is to not frighten her. As soon as she starts moving around, just open the door." He waved his hand. "She'll be gone in a flash."

After Jim left, Mickey sat back on the braided rug and thought about the deer. "You need a name, little one," she murmured, "something beautiful—and wild—and somehow free—"

"How about Morning?" Joel asked. He plopped down beside her, his wet hair neatly combed, his fresh-scrubbed face sparkling with interest.

"Or Fern, maybe," Mickey said, remembering the tall ferns that had brushed her ankles alongside the stream.

Joel nodded. "Ferns are beautiful, wild and free," he agreed.

"But Mornings are more unpredictable." Mickey smiled at the doe. "I have a feeling she is too."

"So Morning it is." Joel turned to address the deer. "Good afternoon, Morning. Nice having you here."

They smiled at each other, their anxiety over the deer temporarily forgotten. But not for long. Morning suddenly struggled to her feet, stood swaying, then dropped back onto the rug.

"Is she all right?" Mickey cried.

A worry line crinkled Joel's forehead. "I—I think so."

They watched her intently for several minutes. Mickey heard a door open and close upstairs.

"What's going on in this place!" Kent roared. "Mud all over the kitchen!"

The doe lurched to her feet. The blanket fell to the floor. Before Joel or Mickey could open the outside door, Morning turned and raced for the only apparent escape—up the stairs, her tiny hooves clattering on the steps.

Joe and Mickey tore after her. The four of them collided at the top of the stairs—Kent, Morning, Joel and Mickey.

A look of bewildered unbelief painted Kent's face as the doe shoved her face into his stomach. "What—"

"Grab her!" Joel cried. But it was too late. Kent had already moved aside.

Her tiny hooves, clattered, then slid on the linoleum. Her legs splayed. Quickly, she recovered her balance and tried to leap. Instead, she collided with a chair, overturning it with a crash.

She slid over the floor onto the carpet in the living room. There she stood, poised to leap through the big picture window.

Joel jumped, grabbing her withers. Then Mickey was at her head. "No, no, Morning," she panted.

Together she and Joel shoved the trembling animal through the kitchen and out the utility entrance. At the door they stepped back, releasing her.

Morning stood quietly, then one big graceful jump and she was off the front steps and running. The gate was closed, but Morning sailed over without effort. The woods before her seemed warm and welcoming.

At its edge she stopped and looked back. Mickey was almost sure she saw a flicker of trust in those large dark eyes. Then Morning flirted her fan-like tail in farewell—like a benediction. Then Morning was gone; the vine maples gathered her into the forest.

Mickey touched Joel's hand. "Do you think we'll ever see her again?" she asked.

But Joel made no reply. They went back into the house.

"Leave you alone just one day and what do we get?" Kent stormed. "Mud—deer—upturned furniture!" His roar turned into a great laugh. He slapped his knee vigorously. "I'll never forget it," he howled, "that deer sliding on the linoleum—and you two kids, hanging on for dear life—dear life—get it? Deer life—"

He grabbed Joel's hand and pumped it furiously. "I

wouldn't have missed it for the world!" He fluffed up Mickey's dark mop. "You're something else, Mickey! Never a dull moment."

He disappeared into the living room, mumbling something about irrational, unpredictable, great show . . .

"I wonder what he'll say when he realizes I borrowed his clothes," Mickey muttered.

A smile twitched Joel's lips. He looked down at his baggy jeans. "I have a feeling he already noticed," he said ruefully.

For the first time Mickey really looked at his clothes. A smile quivered her lips. "Oh, Joel," she gasped. "You do look funny! Those pants and that sweatshirt—"

Suddenly the humor of the situation struck them both. They collapsed in laughter onto the kitchen chairs.

It was there that Loretta found them, the kitchen floor still decorated with mud—the chair upturned.

Joel sobered up in a hurry. He stood up. "Excuse me, Mrs. Middleton. I—"

Mickey caught her breath, suddenly seeing things the way Loretta must see them: unbaked potatoes lying on the counter, mud coating the floor—and telephone. Tracks going into the living room.

"I'm sorry, Loretta. I forgot—"

"It was the deer—" Joel interrupted.

"In the kitchen," Mickey explained.

"A deer in the kitchen?" Loretta repeated. "You'll have to do better than that!"

"There really was, Mrs. Middleton," Joel explained. "Actually it was in the creek—"

"And by the looks of you, so were you?"

Joel nodded. "We all were. But the deer's alive. We got her out—"

"And brought her into the basement. To warm her, you know. But when she heard Kent's voice she suddenly raced up here." Mickey's gesture included both rooms.

"Mickey and I'll clean up," Joel volunteered. "We should have done it sooner, but—"

Mickey hurried for the mop and pail. "You go ahead and relax, Loretta. We'll take care of everything."

Joel grabbed the mop from Mickey's hand. "Sure we will," he agreed.

"I'll put the potatoes into the oven," Mickey exclaimed.

Joel filled the bucket with hot water. "Boy, what a mess!"

"Poor Loretta," Mickey murmured, watching Loretta retreat. "Home to a mess! And what a mess!"

Together the two restored the kitchen to order. Then, while Mickey chopped vegetables for a salad, Joel went in search of Kent. He was back in a few minutes, a warm fleece-lined jacket draped over his arm.

"Kent's neat," he explained as they said their good-byes at the kitchen door. Mickey watched him hurry through the gate and out onto the road.

That night at supper Mickey recounted the afternoon adventure to the entire family. "Wow!" Steve kept repeating. "And I missed it," he concluded. "Phooey on after-school games!"

Later that evening, Mickey brought down the tiny deer carving she'd found in her room. Loretta, alone, an open book on her lap, looked up, smiling. The lamp made a warm circle of light around her, bringing out the rich warm tints in her hair. Mickey stepped toward Loretta, her cupped hand outstretched.

"What do you have there?" Loretta asked.

Mickey sat down on the footstool beside her and opened her hand. "It's a little deer I found in my room."

Loretta gently scooped the small statue into her hand, turning it thoughtfully. "Jami made this," she said softly. "He did things like that."

"I think it's beautiful," Mickey breathed. "The details, the lift of her head. It reminds me of Morning."

She glanced around the room. "Could we keep it on the window ledge? I'd like it there to remind me of—"

But Loretta shook her head. "I'm sorry, Mickey. Even when Jami was with us, Kent wouldn't let me keep them around." She dropped the small deer into Mickey's palm.

"But, why?"

Loretta leaned back and closed her eyes. "Kent's a strange man, Mickey. One idea in his head and he never gives up—never changes.

"Like Jami's carvings; they were so beautiful, showed such promise. But Kent couldn't see it. He thought they were sissy."

"But they aren't," Mickey protested.

Loretta opened her eyes. A slight smile flitted across her face. "I know that, Mickey. But Kent—he wanted so to have a son who was strong, masculine, who'd really amount to something in the world. And all Jami wanted to do was make piles of wood chips in the garage." She sighed. "And now Kent has Steve. Steve tries so hard to measure up. Plays football, soccer, and hates every minute of it. He'd rather be poring over books, dreaming over at the hatchery."

She put the book on the table beside her and stood up. "You can have the deer carving, Mickey. Just keep it in your room."

Mickey looked down at the lovely statue. Beautiful, yet so sad, so very, very sad.

"There's something else in the closet, Loretta. A carved totem pole."

Loretta frowned. "Totem pole? I don't remember any totem pole."

"Come on. I'll show you."

Mickey headed for the stairs, Loretta behind her.

"I put it back into the closet," she explained, opening the door.

Carefully, she lifted it from the shelf and set it on the floor. Loretta looked at it, wonder growing in her eyes. "Why, it's beautiful," she faltered. "But I've never seen it before."

"It was shoved way back on the shelf," Mickey said. "It would have been easy to miss."

Loretta got down on her knees, carefully examining the base. "There's trout down here," she said excitedly, "and water skippers." Her hands moved up the pole. "And here's a leaf drifting over the water."

"It represents Eagle Creek, doesn't it?"

Loretta nodded. "I can see the waterline, too. Right here." She bent closer. "Why, Mickey. I think—"

Loretta laid the pole over her knee and began to twist. The base turned. Mickey gasped.

"Is it hollow?" she cried.

Loretta peered into its rounded darkness. "Nothing inside. Wait. I see something." She put her hand in and pulled out a crumpled piece of paper. "It's a letter," she said in a voice that trembled. Her hands shook as she unfolded it.

"It's from Jami," she whispered, "and it's addressed to the creek!" As she scanned its message, her face drained of color. Her breathing quickened. "Oh, Mickey," she cried, "the poor boy! The poor, poor boy!"

Mickey held out her hand. "May I?" she asked uncertainly.

Loretta nodded. "Go ahead. It was written years ago by a boy who's long since grown—"

Then Loretta put her face in her hands and burst into tears.

Before she could read it, the letter fell from Mickey's hand. Both arms went around Loretta. "Loretta," she whispered, "it's only a letter—"

But Loretta refused to be comforted. "It was my Jami," she cried. "And how we hurt him!"

Awkwardly Mickey patted her shoulder. "It's past, Loretta. Let it go. Let it go—"

The sobs continued, but more softly now. Loretta lifted her head, her eyes flooded, her lashes stuck together in little teepees.

"I'm sorry, Mickey," she said tremulously. "I didn't mean—"

Mickey swallowed hard. "I'm the one who's sorry," she muttered. "I had no idea—"

Loretta smiled, a weak quivering smile that tried to reassure. "Of course you didn't, Mickey. And I—I overreacted." She reached for a tissue from the dresser and blew her nose vigorously. "I'm going downstairs. Thanks for showing me the totem pole. It was something

I needed to see—so I might understand."

After Loretta left, Mickey picked up the note that had fallen on the floor. For a moment she held back, wondering if she should read the words that had so torn Loretta. Then her curiosity overcame her reluctance.

She sat down on the bed, the note before her.

Seven / Shouting—Always Shouting

Dear Eagle Creek,

I loved you, but now I hate you; you've taken my sister, the only one who ever really understood.

My father hates me. He loved HER, because she was fire and vigor and wasn't afraid of anything or anybody.

But you took her. You pressed her beneath you, held her down until she had no more breath, and it was all my fault. I should have leaped in after her. But I was afraid and ran. The others came but it was too late! Too late!

Oh, God, forgive me. Will that day be forever in my memory? Mother standing so still, so wooden, not looking at me, not caring. Dad so angry—shouting, always shouting—

Mickey's eyes stung with unexpected tears. She knew how Kent's rage could strike fear into hearts. And his own son! How could he?

Uncontrolled anger suddenly spilled out of Mickey's

own heart. She drove her fist into her pillow again and again.

"I hate him!" she cried. "All he does is yell and rage. He didn't even try to understand Jami, and now Steve. He should be boiled in oil or—or tar and feathered—"

But should he? Somehow he'd inspired love in Loretta. And he'd been nice about the messy kitchen.

She thought of that morning beneath the cherry tree when he'd told her she could move into her aerie. He'd told her then she could call him "Uncle Kent." Even though the "Uncle" refused to come, he'd still said she could.

Mickey's anger had spent itself as quickly as it had come. She picked up Jami's letter from the floor where it had fallen.

> Once, God, I thought I loved You. But no more. You're mean—poison mean.
>
> I'm running away from you, Eagle Creek. No one cares, not even my family. I'm going far away where no one will ever find me—ever.
>
> Jami
>
> P.S. Good-bye, Eagle Nest. Good-bye. Maybe someday.

The rest of his words were torn from the paper. Mickey looked up, her cheeks wet.

"He'll come back," she whispered. "The stream, this home—they'll pull him back."

She stretched out on the bed, bunching the pillow beneath her head. *How strange,* she thought, *the way he's mixed God and the creek together.*

The house was still, yet Mickey could feel that much

living had once gone on inside its walls. A boy's feet had run up and down the stairs; a sister and brother had called to each other as they played beneath the birches. There was only quiet now.

Mickey was motionless for a long time, staring at the totem pole with a slight frown on her face, eyes narrowed, jaw firm. Her thoughts were confused, disconnected, roaming back to Jami's note.

Once she said aloud, "God—poison mean? I don't know much about Him, but He can't be, can He?" Later, in a puzzled half-whisper, "I think Jami knew God, sort of, maybe even like Joel does. But hurt made his thoughts get all mixed up." Finally, "I wish I could have known Jami. I really do."

After a while she got up and began to prepare for bed. She donned flannel pajamas and brushed her hair until it gleamed. Before she snuggled under the blanket, she picked up the letter, folded it carefully, and put it back inside the totem pole, then placed the totem pole on the window ledge beside the deer and fox. The three seemed to go together.

The eagle with lowered wings, the timid deer, and the dashing trout watched over that night, flavoring her dreams with a touch of the wild. A running deer came closer—closer. Just as she reached out her hand, it dashed away—only to reappear some distance away, nibbling grass in a field of sun-drenched daisies.

In the morning Mickey worked alone in the rain-soaked garden. She vigorously attacked a great overgrown bridal wreath, hewing it down, digging out its huge roots. Her face grew flushed and damp while last year's leaves clung to her flannel shirt and her hands grew gooey with mud.

After clearing the root hole of old root strands, she shoved dirt into it, smoothing it with a rake. A robin trilled its amazement from the cherry tree—or was it anticipating lunch from the soft, damp earth?

It was fun to poke among frail pansy plants, then to stand back and look at their altered appearance. A drift of blossoms reminiscent of winter snow blew toward her. Loretta came out, and they admired the freshly prepared corner together.

After a warm, sudsy shower and a hot soup lunch, Mickey rambled down to the creek. A great curiosity rose in her as she fingered green lichens and caressed great shaggy mosses. Was the totem pole changing her? Or was the deer? Or was Jami's note?

Mickey wasn't sure. She only knew that something deep inside her seemed to have been kindled into flame. She had to learn about crayfish and goldfinches, robins and deer, mayflowers and trilliums.

She tried to express herself that night when the family gathered for supper in the warm kitchen.

Loretta looked up. "Lichens?" she asked. "What about them?"

"I'd just like to find out more about how they grow—what they're called. And the stream life—the little nymphs and the dragonflies. I found some big white bumpy things growing on a log, too. I wondered what they were."

"Counches," Steve explained. "They're parasites."

"You sure do know your biology," Mickey said with some astonishment. "I've never heard of counches."

"I like science, and our teacher knows all about the plants and animals in the local forests."

"Anyway," Mickey continued, "I saw a bird flitting around in the vine maples. I'd never seen it before. It had a red head, and it appeared to be looking for something."

"We have the *Audubon* and the *National Geographic* magazines," Steve suggested. "I've learned a lot from them. I'll get them for you after dinner."

Kent put down his fork. "They teach that sort of thing at the high school here," he explained. "When you go this fall you ought to check into some of those courses."

School—of course she knew she'd have to go back. The thought made knots roll up in her stomach. Why did Kent have to mention it now? School—she'd only be a junior when she should be a senior.

Her caseworker's words twisted in her mind. "Since it's so close to year's end and you're so hopelessly behind, we think you might as well stay out until fall. A new start . . ."

And it was my running off that did it, Mickey thought, *my sheer stupidity.* Her face burned.

Loretta was steering the conversation into smoother channels. "They have bird and tree identification books at the library in town. Maybe that would help. We could stop there some afternoon."

Steve looked at Mickey intently. "I could bring you some from the school library, too."

Mickey mumbled her thanks and excused herself. Later that evening she was pleasantly surprised to answer a knock at the door and to find Tam's smiling face.

The two girls sat on the living room carpet, Steve's *National Geographics* spread around them, their Coke bottles positioned precariously close by.

"Do they really have classes at school that tell you about things like trees, plants, wildflowers and wildlife?" Mickey asked hesitantly.

"Well, that's not really my speciality," Tam said, lifting her Coke to her lips. "But Joel took biology last year. He had a lot of fun making a wildflower scrapbook with pressed flowers. I remember some of his diagrams of plant parts, too.

"Now me, I'm more into fun things, like ceramics and home economics." She looked thoughtful. "You know, Mickey, you and Joel sort of like the same things."

Mickey pulled a magazine closer. "Look at this picture of Mt. St. Helens," she exclaimed. "Isn't it spectacular?"

But Tam wasn't paying attention. "I wish you'd go to church with us," she said unexpectedly.

Mickey put the magazine down. "Why?"

Tam set her Coke beside her. "I think Joel would like to date you," she confided, "but he's funny. He has this idea he shouldn't because you're not a Christian." She tossed her head. "Now, I'm a Christian too, but I don't feel that way. I'd date a fellow who wasn't one if I knew his moral standards were the same as mine—" She smiled at Mickey. "And I know you're a good person, Mickey."

A vision of her rage at Kent's treatment of his sons exploded in Mickey's mind. "Oh, no, I'm not, Tam. I'm not good at all—"

Tam's eyebrows quirked inquiringly. But Mickey was silent, the only sound in the room was the rustle of magazine pages, and the nearby roar of the creek.

"Maybe I should—" she said after a moment.

"Should what?"

"Go to church." She changed the subject abruptly. "Now these are the kind of pictures I go for; close-ups of tiny things. See those red and black ants, and the round bright eyes on that jumping spider?"

After awhile Tam left, but Mickey lingered over the magazines. The bustling world of life on a rock ledge captivated her imagination. *What tiny creatures live there!* It would be that way at the creek, too, only different . . .

Loretta brought her back to reality. "Telephone, Mickey!"

Mickey, a magazine still clutched in her hand, hurried into the kitchen. She picked up the receiver.

"Mickey, it's me, Joel—What are you doing?"

"Right now?" She giggled suddenly. "I'm talking to you—but I was looking at magazines. Steve gave me a stack of *National Geographics* and some old copies of the *Audubon*."

"Good, aren't they? But what I was calling about— would you like to go with Tam and me to the May Day celebration at our high school? It's always sort of special, with marching bands and Maypole dances. It would give you a chance to meet the kids, too."

May Day celebration—marching bands—with Joel?

Tam's words intruded into her wildly singing thoughts. *"I think Joel would like to date you, but he's funny. He has this idea he shouldn't because you're not a Christian."*

"I—I." Mickey started.

"I wish you'd go to church with us." Tam had said. *"I know you're a good person, Mickey."*

"Are you there, Mickey?" Joel asked.

"Yes, yes, of course. I was just thinking. I'd like that. And Joel—do you suppose you could pick me up Sunday morning so I could go to church with you and Tam?"

Afterwards Mickey wondered why she'd said it. But it was too late now. She was committed. Somehow, deep inside, she was glad.

Eight / People Are More Important

"Tam said a dress," Mickey muttered as she got ready for church. She pushed several hangers in her closet aside, carefully examining each outfit.

There weren't many; a slimming navy blue that made her dark hair look darker, a soft pink with feathery swirls, a paisley print in reds and purples . . .

She chose a long-sleeved white blouse with eyelet trim and a soft, dark blue skirt with simple lines. After she had washed her hair and blown it dry, she had to admit she did look nice.

The look in Joel's eyes told her she did, too. And Tam was quick to pick up on it. "You look nice dressed up, Mickey," she approved.

"You do too," Mickey said quickly, noting Tam's beige skirt, with the smart narrow red belt.

Joel looked decidedly out of character in dark brown cords and a striped tan velour pullover with a V-neck. His red-brown hair looked curlier than ever.

"I'm so glad you could come," he said as he backed the car around and headed up the hill.

Mickey chose to ignore Tam's sudden giggle. "It was nice of you to pick me up," she said sedately.

"How has your week been?" Joel asked, glancing at her from across Tam, who was tightly wedged between them.

"Never a dull moment," Mickey said. "Let's see . . . Yesterday I visited Jim over at the hatchery. The day before that—" She giggled. "I practiced casting down by the open space where Loretta has her little trees growing.

"And I've read a lot." She didn't say where she'd read though. Those hours she'd spent perched on the limb outside the window were somehow special— private. It had been a different world tucked high above the ground, enclosed in the tree's white-scented arms.

Sadness wafted through her. The blossoms were almost gone, drifting away in the lazy warm days following the rain.

Church that morning was a jumbled confusion of strange faces, unfamiliar surroundings. But she liked Mr. Hoffman, the Sunday school teacher.

He made her feel comfortable right away with his friendly, "You came with the Brentwoods? So glad you did!"

She listened intently to his words. He was teaching from the vision of the prophet, Isaiah. He made it come alive: the prostrate prophet, the flaming coal, a God of glory seated on His throne.

She looked across at Joel. He listened with quiet concentration, a slight frown creasing his forehead. Mr. Hoffman's voice faded as she watched Joel; a stray sunbeam wandered through his reddish curls, highlighting bits of hidden gold.

He caught the intent of her gaze and looked toward

her. His smile flashed. Mickey flushed and lowered her eyes.

During the discussion that followed, her attention was caught. How eager the class was. How excited!

"I'm reading Isaiah like you suggested we do, Mr. Hoffman," Joel said, "not to understand the vision especially, but to see how Isaiah saw his God."

Mr. Hoffman nodded. "Did you notice how many times Isaiah called his God the Lord of hosts?"

"Yes," Joel said. "But it was chapter twenty-eight that showed me even more about what my God is like. I wrote, 'My Lord is . . .' as a starter, then listed everything I could find that described Him."

He flipped through the pages of his Bible and drew out a piece of paper. "My Lord is a crown of glory, a diadem of beauty, a tested stone, a precious cornerstone, a sure foundation, my teacher and instructor, the Lord of hosts, wonderful in counsel, excellent in working!" He lifted his head. "Isn't that beautiful? And it's all in chapter twenty-eight!"

A small, slim girl leaned forward. "The Lord of hosts caught my attention, too. I looked it up in my concordance and found a verse in Micah 4:4 that really impressed me: 'But they shall sit every man under his vine and under his fig tree; and none shall make them afraid; for the mouth of the Lord of hosts hath spoken it.' "

She lifted her head. "God's people had been taken away from their homes by this time and were living in strange lands. How they wanted to be back in their own homes. And God, the mighty Lord of hosts, understood their heart's desires and promised each of them a place of their own."

A sudden yearning welled up inside Mickey. The girl continued. "Understanding how much God loved them makes me realize He loves me and cares about me in the same way."

Afterwards in the foyer, Joel introduced Mickey to his parents. "Mom and Dad, this is Mickey, our friend living with the Middletons."

"Nice to meet you, Mickey." William Brentwood shook her hand warmly. "I'm Bill, and this is my wife Eileen. We're happy you could come this morning with Joel and Tam. They tell us you enjoy the outdoors—animals and Eagle Creek."

Mickey could see Joel's kind eyes in his father's. And Joel's gentle smile was a copy of his mother's.

"Yes," Mickey responded. "You should have been there the other day when Joel and I rescued Morning, the deer, from the creek. What was funny was when she dashed upstairs and nearly jumped through the window. Joel caught her just in time."

"You certainly had an adventure," Bill chuckled, "and I'm sure there'll be more. Let's go in and sit down for the service."

Joel, Mickey and Tam had barely settled themselves in the car when Tam turned eagerly to Mickey. "Did you like it?"

"Yes, I did," Mickey confessed. "Especially the Sunday school class. It almost made me want to go home and start reading Isaiah—and I'm not a Bible reader."

Tam nodded. "I felt that way last winter when we were studying the book of John. If you've never read the Bible much, Mickey, that's a good place to start."

Joel turned on the ignition. "John's gospel made me appreciate Jesus in a new way," Joel continued, "as the Good Shepherd, the light of the world, the bread of life.

"Now I understand why Mr. Hoffman had us study it before Isaiah. It makes the majesty and sovereignty of God easier to understand when we know that His only Son later walked on our earth."

Mickey mulled over Joel's words when she got home. She found a Bible in an open-shelved bookcase beside the fireplace. As she pulled it out, she spied behind the bookcase a folded piece of yellowed paper between the baseboard and the wall. Almost subconsciously she picked up a pencil, squiggling its tip beneath the board.

She tried to draw it out several times. But each time it slid past her eager fingers. Then she had it. She unfolded it.

The words sprang out at her:

> If you really love me and can forgive me for not being the person you want me to be, I'll be at Paul Larson's house at 103 S. Aaron Rd., in Spring Valley, California.
>
> Love,
> Jami

Mickey's first impulse was to show the note to Loretta. She jumped to her feet, then stood still.

That note was written nine years ago, she thought. *How would reading it now help matters? How would it make Loretta feel?*

"I'll write Jami myself," Mickey decided, "maybe, just maybe—"

Slowly she refolded the note and slid it into the Bible. "Poor Jami, poor Kent and Loretta. I wonder if anyone ever found this note." The conviction grew within her that they hadn't.

That night Mickey wrote two letters—one to the long-lost Jami, another to the unknown Paul Larson of Spring Valley.

Afterwards she opened the Bible to the Gospel of John and began to read. "In the beginning was the Word and the Word was with God, and the Word was God. . . ."

The next week raced by. Loretta was planning a wedding shower for Lucille's daughter, and the house had to be perfectly clean for the big evening.

Mickey and Loretta vacuumed floors, washed windows, polished furniture and scoured sinks. Loretta spent hours in the kitchen planning the games and preparing the punch and cake.

Mickey stood admiring the finished product. The cake was beautiful, shaped like a bell, garnished with pink roses and tiny silver leaves.

Like May Day, Mickey thought, *with flowers—fun*. Anticipation rushed through her.

Loretta smiled at her. "Mickey, the punch bowl's stored in our closet. Would you mind getting it down for me and washing it?"

Mickey nodded and hurried into Kent and Loretta's bedroom. She opened the closet door. The punch bowl, wrapped in clear plastic, was on the top shelf.

As she reached for it, the vase beside it started to topple. Mickey gasped and tried to catch it. But she was too late. The vase crashed on the edge of a chair, shattering into a dozen pieces.

"Oh, no!" she cried.

The door opened. Kent stood looking at her. Mickey's insides trembled. She bent to pick up the glass with unsteady fingers.

Kent stared at her coldly. "What do you think you're doing?" he demanded. "That's my mother's vase you've destroyed! Have you no sense?"

"I—I—" Mickey blurted, "I didn't mean to! I—"

"Didn't mean too! Of course you didn't mean to. But you did!"

Mickey looked up. She felt her throat tighten. Her eyes blurred. "I'm sorry," she whispered. "I was just getting the punch bowl down. It was an accident—"

Kent wheeled away from her, the door slamming behind him. Mickey swallowed hard. Through her tears she noticed Margot's picture smiling at her.

Sudden anger surged through her. "*You* wouldn't do something like this, would you, Margot. *You* weren't clumsy. He loved *you*—just the way you were!"

Mickey leaped to her feet, bitterness rushing through her. *What would it be like to be the much loved, protected daughter of the house? To really belong?*

On impulse she turned Margot's picture to the wall, then ran out the door. She almost collided with Loretta. But Mickey rushed past her through the living room and out the front door. Almost without thinking she turned toward the hatchery.

She'd look at the fish, the little ones. They wouldn't care that she wasn't Margot, that she didn't belong.

She leaned over the runway, peering into the water. There was a light step behind her. A hand dropped to her shoulder.

"I didn't mean to," Mickey whispered. The tears,

which had been threatening her, started to fall. She put her face inside her hands.

"Why—why, Little Bunny, what is it? What's hurting you so?"

Startled, Mickey uncovered her face. Jim looked down at her, his dark blue eyes filled with compassion. *Strange*, she thought, *his eyes are the same color as Kent's*. But Kent's were like an impenetrable wall while Jim's were like wells of refreshing water.

"The vase," Mickey whispered. "I broke their vase. It belonged to his mother."

Jim nodded, his eyes thoughtful. "That's bad," he agreed, "but not the end of the world."

"But you don't know!" Mickey cried. She was suddenly silent. She had no words to explain the mixed-up feelings tangled inside her.

But Jim seemed to understand. "It's hard," he murmured, "hard when you never feel like your best is good enough—"

"Margot—she was everything to him—"

A startled look flickered across his face. "And you?"

"I'm nothing. Not their daughter, not even their friend—right now."

"But you are, Mickey!" he exclaimed. "You are a very special person in your own right. I know things look awful to you right now. You've hurt someone without meaning to. You've broken something that's probably irreplaceable—"

The sad, wistful look she'd noticed before flitted over his face. "But remember—people are much more important than things. He'll get over it. He really will."

Mickey brushed the tears from her eyes. "Do you

really think so?" she asked.

"Yes, I do, Little Bunny. I really do."

His words distracted Mickey from her problem. "Why did you call me that?" she asked curiously. "Little Bunny—it makes me think of the name I call you."

Jim smiled. "And that's—"

A flush rose into Mickey's cheeks. Her lips parted slightly. "It's—It's—Peter Rabbit—"

"Peter Rabbit! Isn't he the little rabbit that got into Mr. McGregor's garden?"

Mickey nodded eagerly. "He disobeyed his mother and ran away to nibble the lettuce. And Mr. McGregor came after him with the hoe."

"But why do you call me that?"

"Just—just—because—"

"Well, if you call me Peter Rabbit, then I can keep on calling you Little Bunny. Right?"

Mickey laughed. "Right!" She looked toward the pink house. "I should go back—Peter Rabbit."

"I agree. They'll feel badly." A frown creased his forehead. "Face up to it now. Don't let it get out of hand." He shoved her gently. "Get now."

Mickey started to leave, then stopped. "Peter Rabbit, I want you to know that rabbits are kind, gentle. You're that kind of person." Then Mickey was running.

Loretta met her at the door.

"Mickey!" she exclaimed. "It's all right. Vases are nice, but girls—daughters are better."

"But Kent—"

Loretta brushed her comment aside. "He'll get over it. Of course he felt badly, but he'd be the first to agree, people are more important than things."

As Mickey hurried into the kitchen behind Loretta, she thought about Loretta's words. Strange. Peter Rabbit had said the very same thing.

Nine / May Day and Mrs. Morton

The morning of the long-awaited May Day celebration dawned clear.

Like a new golden chick just hatched from the egg, Mickey thought, as she brushed her hair to shining perfection and donned her new outfit of soft-brushed green corduroy. Butterflies suddenly fluttered in her stomach. "My school debut," she muttered.

Loretta turned as Mickey entered the kitchen. "It looks nice," she approved, "and worth all those hours we spent searching for it." A teasing smile stole across her lips; her gray eyes gleamed. "How about fixing a bouquet for the breakfast table? After all, it is May Day."

Mickey nodded, her thoughts not really on flowers and old, worn-out traditions. She took the shears Loretta handed her and went outside. On the porch, she almost stepped on a delicate arrangement of snowy lily of the valley mingled with fern fronds, tucked inside a basket.

Mickey gasped and knelt, burying her face in their enticing fragrance. Her nose brushed the edge of a tiny note tucked inside. Wondering, Mickey drew it out. Her name was on the front. Inside the note proclaimed only two words: "You're special."

Mickey took a deep breath and hugged it to her heart. Suddenly the old traditions of May baskets and flowers didn't seem ridiculous at all!

She hurried inside, holding the bouquet in front of her. "It's for me!" she cried. "You knew!"

Loretta laughed and hugged her, careful not to crush the flowers. "Of course! I almost knocked it over when I opened the door." She smiled knowingly at Mickey. "I thought May baskets went out years ago. Somebody must be reviving old traditions."

"I don't know who they're from," Mickey explained, "but I want to share." She set the basket in the middle of the table and stood back, admiring their spring beauty.

"Aha—flowers for Mickey!" Kent exclaimed as he and Steve came into the room. He winked at her quizzically as he sat down.

Steve cocked his eyebrows. "Joel?"

Mickey shook her head as she too sat down. "I don't know." She felt exquisite pink tint her cheeks, contrasting with her dark green jacket, her brown eyes and hair.

For the first time in her life she felt beautiful—really beautiful, the torment of breaking the vase far away. She slipped her fingers beneath her napkin and pinched her leg to be sure she was really awake.

May Day was everything Joel and Tam had said it would be—only more: the flower-decked court with the queen, her maidens and their escorts, the marching bands, gymnastic teams tumbling on mats, leaping pom-pom girls.

The girls' P.E. classes had combined to form a marching formation. Figure eights and geometric designs formed and reformed with neat precision. Eagerly, Mickey searched for Tam's long legs and red hair. She spotted her at last, shoulders and legs moving rhythmically, not missing a beat.

The Maypole dance was next. Freshman girls in long, floating pastel dresses, gracefully dipped and swayed, somehow managing to artfully weave the long streamers around each pole.

"I did that when I was a freshman," Tam explained, sliding onto the bleacher seat beside Mickey. She'd changed out of her white blouse and navy shorts; and her crisp bright hair, freshly combed, caught bits of sunshine.

"The relays and games are next," she said as the boys removed the poles to the edge of the field. "Enjoying it?"

"Yes, I am," Mickey replied. "The kids are friendly, too."

There was a sudden hush in the crowd and a commotion on the flower-decked court. Mickey saw a clown with a long, sad face climb the steps and begin to carefully dust the podium. His suit was bright red and yellow, and over his shoulder drifted a purple polka-dotted cape.

The princesses and their escorts drew back, the girls giggling, as he fruitlessly tried dusting each one with his large feather duster. But the sad-faced clown was undaunted, waving his duster as he stepped before the queen. He raised his duster once, twice, then dropped it on the ground. The cape slid from his shoulders in one smooth motion, and with a flourish, he laid it before the queen.

Her arm rotated. The bouquet she carried flew through the air. The clown caught it in one hand and whirled in a circle of delight.

The band crashed forth triumphant music. Around and around he danced, the court following suit. Then the pom-pom girls and the spectators joined them. The field vibrated with color and movement.

"Until the clown came, I thought the Maypole was best," Mickey commented to Joel and Tam as Joel drove her home.

Joel cast her a startled look. Tam threw back her head and laughed.

"What—what's so funny?" Mickey stammered.

"It's just that—that—Can we tell her, Joel?"

"We're not laughing at you, Mickey," Joel explained. "It's just that I'm the clown, that's all."

"No one at school has guessed it yet," Tam gasped. "It's unbelievable!"

Mickey turned and stared at Joel a long studying moment. "I think I might have," she said softly, "if I'd thought about it enough. You did an awfully good job, Joel. What made you do it?"

Joel smiled at her. "Something inside me, I guess. I started last summer, helping with the Bible school kids at church. They loved it."

Tam bounced between them. "I even filled in for him one day, and they never even guessed. It's something we can both do." She made a face at her brother. "But he works harder at it than I do."

After they let Tam out at a friend's house, Joel and Mickey rode in silence. *What an unusual mixture of talents he has*, Mickey thought. *Tam says he plays football in the fall—that he's one of their top players. And he fishes. Now this. I wonder if he'd be any good at finding missing persons ...*

"What are you thinking?" Joel asked.

"Nothing. Nothing much that is. Except—Joel, you seem to be involved in a lot of things."

"Shoot," he said, "what's bothering you?"

"It's the Middletons' missing son," she said slowly. "It started with a totem pole—then a letter—and last week, a note ..."

Quickly she recounted Loretta's story and how she'd become involved by her desire to move into the upstairs bedroom.

"Aside from the letters you've already written, I don't think there's much you can do, Mickey," Joel said when she'd finished. "It happened so long ago."

Mickey nodded uncertainly. "I wish I could do more—for Steve's sake. He always seems to be struggling, never measuring up. So quiet—and Kent is always yelling at him."

They pulled into the driveway. Mickey started to get out, but Joel restrained her with a hand on her shoulder.

"I've something—" He reached into the backseat, "for you, Mickey." Gently he laid the queen's bouquet on her lap.

"Oh!" Mickey cried in startled wonderment. She buried her face in the delicate rosebuds, the white carnations, the dainty baby's breath. "It's beautiful!"

She lifted her head and looked at him. Such tenderness there was around his mouth, such quiet caring reflecting Mickey's precious moment. And then, "It's Mrs. Morton," she said, "my caseworker is here."

Quickly she pushed open the door. "Good-bye, Joel.

And thank you—for a wonderful day—" she touched a rosebud, "these wonderful flowers."

She watched the two cars maneuver around each other. Then Joel's green Chevrolet wended up the hill, and Mrs. Morton was beside her on the path.

Mickey held the flowers out to her. "Aren't they beautiful!"

But Mrs. Morton paid no attention. Her heavy face was lined with care, her thoughts obviously on other things. "I don't know how to tell you this, Mickey . . . but . . . Let's go inside."

Mickey frowned. A cold chill circled her heart. She shivered.

Loretta met them at the door. She started to exclaim over the flowers Mickey held, then stopped. "There's a vase beneath the sink."

Loretta and Mrs. Morton went into the living room. Mickey found the green knobby container and turned on the faucet. She heard the low murmur of their voices, worried voices.

"Her mother—I don't know how to tell her."

The water ran over Mickey's hands. She turned it off and rushed into the living room.

"What is it?" she cried.

Loretta put both arms around her. "It's all right, Mickey," she reassured, "just unexpected."

Mickey looked intently at Loretta's face, Loretta's lips tremulous, her dark gray eyes shiny with—unshed tears?

Mrs. Morton came directly to the point. "We found your mother, Mickey," she said. "Actually, she found us."

"But—but—" Mickey cried.

"She's very ill, my dear. She had a nurse query our office. She'd like to see you."

Mickey licked her lips. "Where is she?"

"At a hospital in Portland. She's registered as Joanne Cochran." Mrs. Morton stood up. "Whether or not you wish to see her is entirely up to you. If you want to go I'll take you. If not—" She spread her short stubby fingers wide, "I'll send her word."

Mickey walked to the window. The delicate green veil that had seemed to float over the alders and vine maples was deeper now. The tender new leaves moved in the quiet breeze. Beyond, the creek flashed.

Mother's eyes were like the stream, Mickey thought. *Why did she leave me? How could she?*

Loretta came over and stood beside her. "If you want to see her, I'll go with you."

Mickey shook her head. "No. If I go—I'll go alone."

But did she want to? *She left me when I needed her,* her insides cried. *What right does she have to come back into my life now?*

Abruptly she turned to Loretta. "What do you think I should do?" she asked.

Loretta's lips whitened. She took a deep breath. "You're old enough to make your own decision, Mickey. But," she continued relentlessly, "if you refuse to see her, it may be something you'll regret the rest of your life. She *is* your mother, even though she failed you utterly."

"I'll go then." She broke away from Loretta's steadying arm.

"I'd get a sweater if I were you, Mickey," Mrs. Morton suggested. "It's getting cool."

Mickey nodded. Upstairs she pulled a white cardigan off a hanger, then stepped to the window and leaned out. Peaceful days—busy hours—now this.

She clattered down the stairs. "I've decided not to go," she said. "Maybe later—maybe never."

Without another word she turned and left the room. The dark fir trees at the edge of the garden beckoned to her. She went deep into the woods.

It was a while before she noticed the firs murmuring in the wind, a chattering squirrel, a dove cooing far in the distance. Then a blue jay set up his own raucous calling, flashing from limb to limb.

Mickey found a rotten stump in a clearing and sat down. A deer, its ears trembling, stopped at the edge of her vine maple-trimmed meadow and looked at her. Mickey drew in her breath. It flicked its white tail and bounded away.

A sense of startled awe wrapped itself around her spirit. *Morning—could it have been Morning?*

Mickey fell into a daydream. A tiny elf, not much bigger than a drop of water, clambered onto a tiny mushroom. Another swung from a moss-draped limb. They were calling to Morning that Mickey wouldn't hurt her, that she cared.

Mickey got up and went deeper into the woods. Here the tightly interwoven branches overhead were a canopy.

Mickey could picture it in the winter, the topside of the canopy lashed by fierce wind and rain—while beneath, the ferns and bushes would scarcely move.

Vaguely, she wondered what lived up there. Most of the birds she had observed seemed to be building their nests in the thickets or even on the ground. An unseen creature scuttled beneath a clump of hazelbrush—going home.

Quite suddenly Mickey knew what she must do.

Ten / Mother

"I've decided I need to see my mother." Mickey stood in the kitchen, a weary figure with soft, tangled hair and dirt on her shoes.

Loretta turned from the biscuits she was cutting. A slight frown creased her forehead, her pupils narrowed, and the irises, dark gray and thoughtful, narrowed and sharpened with them.

"I'm glad," she said quietly.

Mickey pulled a rosebud and a tangled bit of baby's breath from the vase she'd left on the counter. "I could take these—"

"That would be nice." Loretta wiped her fingers on a paper towel and put her hand on Mickey's shoulder. "You've made a difficult decision, Mickey, and I'm proud of you." She moved away. "I'll drive you in after dinner."

The long ride into Portland was a haze in Mickey's mind. Her fingers clutched her rose as she dully observed the maze of bridges, the lights reflecting off the

Willamette River ...

Loretta left her at the curb of the busy hospital, promising to meet her in the waiting room after she'd found a parking place.

Mickey spoke briefly to a busy woman behind a desk. The elevator claimed her, then the long hallway. She walked past hurrying nurses, peered at numbers over bustling wards, caught glimpses of white-gowned patients, some in beds, others wandering aimlessly.

A man with protruding tubes had been left on a stretcher outside a crowded ward—asleep—but, nonetheless, all alone. Mickey's throat suddenly ached. Her eyes burned. She hurried quickly away.

The number 337 blazed at her. A salty taste filled her mouth; cold sweat broke out on the palms of her hands. She had to force herself not to grab her stomach, which had become a hard, uncooperative lump.

She stepped through the door, her chin held high. "Mother—"

The dark-haired woman looking out the window turned toward her. Mickey was only conscious of her eyes—big, dark, questioning, with shadows beneath.

She held out her hand uncertainly. "Michelle?"

Mickey stepped over to the bed. She swallowed hard. "Mother?"

They looked at each other—a long, searching look that somehow failed to span the missing years.

The woman licked her lips, then brushed her hair nervously off her forehead. *It's ugly hair*, Mickey thought irrelevantly, *short, uneven—*

"I—I'm glad you came. I—"

"I didn't know where you were," Mickey explained

needlessly. "You never wrote—or called—"

The long thin hands grabbed the edge of the blanket. "I was here—here in Portland."

"I—I tried to find you when I was little," Mickey whispered. "How could you? And my brothers—Kevin, Alan—where are they?"

Her eyes shifted around the room. "The last I heard Kevin was in Sandy," she muttered. "He never writes."

"And Alan?"

The haunted eyes returned to Mickey's face. "He didn't turn out so good," she said. "He's in a special school—here in town." She twisted her fingers helplessly around the sheet. "I'm not a good woman," she whispered, "but I did love you."

"I tried to find you," Mickey repeated, "and all the time you were here in Portland." It was a statement, not a question.

"I used my maiden name," she explained. She leaned back on her pillow. "You never knew, Michelle, but the boys weren't really Strands. I didn't even know who their fathers were.

"That's why I left you. I didn't deserve you. Your real father did."

"But he left me, too!" Mickey cried. "And before he did, we just went from place to place." A vision of sagging porches, ancient gas stoves and hooks to hang her clothes on rose before her. A bitter taste filled her mouth. "Then one day he was gone—"

She fell silent. It had started then, the round of foster homes. She saw herself, a plain, sullen girl, not quite belonging in any of them.

"When I was twelve they told me he'd died." The

silence deepened. She remembered that she'd cried a little that night, not because of the dirt and unhappiness he'd led her through, but because in some way she didn't understand, she had known he loved her in his funny, inadequate way. Like the day he'd put his arms around her when she'd run away from her fourth grade class, the Christmas morning she'd found the big white teddy bear at the foot of her bed . . .

Her mother's hand reached out and touched hers. "I'm sorry," she whispered, "but you're my baby girl. Can't you forgive me—love me—a little?"

Mickey suddenly fell to her knees beside the bed, covering her face in the bedspread. "I don't know!" she cried. "A tiny piece inside me says I do love you. But I just don't know!" She lifted her head. "I never let anyone call me Michelle because you were the only one who ever did—back then. And it was your own special name for me.

"But I can't understand why you would leave me. Just because the boys weren't Daddy's—"

"I had to get away," the woman whispered. "I couldn't stand those four walls—no money. And before that, the shouting—"

Get away! It was stirring inside Mickey. *Get away!* She leaped to her feet and looked down at her mother. "I have to go now." She tried to say "Mother," but the word stuck in her throat.

The woman clutched at Mickey's hands. Suddenly Mickey remembered her rose. "Here," she said, thrusting it into the sick woman's hand.

Then Mickey was running—out the door—down the hall. She almost collided with Loretta, who was hurrying toward her, an anxious look on her face. "Mickey—"

"I've seen her already," Mickey exclaimed. "Let's go—"

The evening air cooled her burning cheeks. She took a deep breath, then turned to Loretta.

"She's sick—really sick. I can see that. But Loretta, it was so awful!"

Loretta grabbed her arm and hurried alongside her. "We're parked over here."

Once inside the car Mickey buried her face in her hands and burst into tears. "I'm not crying just because she's sick," she wailed, "but because everything is so different from what I imagined meeting my mother would be. I had such dreams. All she wanted was for me to forgive her because she left me, and I—I found out I couldn't!"

Loretta's hand groped for hers. "It's all right, Mickey. Everything will be all right."

But it wasn't. All night Mickey tossed and turned. A tangled web of feeling kept tugging inside her; resentment, pity, then pain.

"She should never have asked me to come," she whispered into the darkness. "She had no right to spoil my day." Then later, "But she is my mother. I should love her. But I don't."

As dawn interrupted the darkness, she lay in bed and watched the sunlight gradually lighten the wide-winged eagle, the tiny deer, the queen's bouquet she'd placed on her dressing table. *Joel*, she thought, *oh, Joel . . .*

After breakfast, Mickey slipped away to the fish hatchery. Perhaps if she could talk to Peter Rabbit, he would understand.

Jim took one look at her as she stood in the doorway. He put down the tray he was carrying and came over to her. "What's up, Little Bunny?"

Slowly, haltingly, Mickey's story tumbled out. The wonderful May Day morning, the arrival of her caseworker, and the awfulness of facing the woman who'd left her poured out of her. Together Mickey and Jim left the building, walking past the runways and the holding tank. They stopped at the bridge and leaned over the railing, neither one seeing the dashing, laughing creek beneath them.

"I don't see why it had to happen now—why it had to be so different than I'd dreamed."

A question formed in Jim's eyes.

"Sometimes I'd imagine that she'd come searching for me," Mickey explained, "that we'd see each other and everything would be magically forgotten. Other times I'd pretend I'd meet her and quietly tell her what an awful woman she was for failing me and my father. I'd shout that she had no right to run off with my brothers—

"But lately, I've been thinking less about her. Somehow I was beginning to want to get on with my own life. Then there she was. When I saw her, it wasn't like anything I'd ever imagined. I hardly recognized her; her hair was short, and she didn't seem the same at all."

She propped her elbows on the railing and held her face between her hands. "I think what bothers me most now is that I see something of me in her, the me I don't like—always running from what's painful or hard. And yet sometimes, I just long to go back—to that little, yellow house."

She lifted her face. "Did you ever have a place like that, Jim? A place that was sheltered and happy?"

Jim nodded slowly. "Mine was high up in a treetop. I felt so secure and happy up there—"

"Mine was underneath a snowball bush. My brothers and I would crawl inside and be in a world apart, our own little world. Nothing could hurt us there, not our mother, not our father.

"Sometimes Mother would call me and I'd pretend I didn't hear her. Then she'd call again, 'Michelle! Michelle Ann Strand!'"

Jim looked at her, understanding dawning in his dark blue eyes. "Is that why you never let anyone else call you that?"

"I—I—" Further self-understanding dawned inside Mickey's heart. "Yes."

Jim put his arm around her shoulders. "Michelle," he said softly. "Michelle. It's a lovely name."

"But a hurting name," Mickey cried. Her chin trembled. "Whenever someone calls me Michelle, I remember the rejection, the pain. Do you think it will ever go away?"

Jim's hand tightened, and Mickey looked at him. His eyes searched the water, but Mickey knew he saw something far beyond.

"I don't have the answer to that one, Mickey," he said at last. "Will the past always follow us and haunt us if we keep running from it?"

His arm dropped from her shoulders, and he turned away. Mickey watched him—a lonely, dark-haired man, the weight of his thoughts bending his shoulders. Her

Peter Rabbit—walking away.

A sharp pain pulled up the corners of her mouth. "Oh, Peter Rabbit," she murmured, "are you running away from something too?"

Eleven / Away! Away!

"Who do you know in Spring Valley?" Kent asked, dropping a letter beside Mickey's plate.

A hot flush dyed Mickey's cheeks as she picked it up. Kent, Loretta and Steve looked at her expectantly.

"No one really. Just a friend of a friend—sort of." She slid the letter into her shirt pocket and smiled at them.

"I've been reading Steve's *Audubon* magazines," she said, eager to change the subject. "Did you know that no two robins sing exactly the same way?"

"What do you mean?" Steve asked, his blue eyes flashing interest.

"Each robin varies its song, puts phrases together differently. Even an individual robin will sing as many as ten different songs, depending somewhat on the time of day."

Loretta laid down her fork. "I never knew that. It's fascinating, isn't it?"

Mickey nodded. "I think it's true, too. When I wake up early, it seems I can identify different robin tunes.

And one night I was sure I heard a robin sing in the rain. It was so sad, and yet so beautiful."

"Don't you sleep well, Button Nose?" Kent asked.

Mickey shrugged. "Of course I do. But sometimes I wake up early, even in the middle of the night."

It was true. Restlessness in her new home, troubled thoughts about her new family, her mother, Peter Rabbit, and even Jami and Margot kept her from sleeping soundly. Lying in bed, she'd listen to the birds' riotous early morning chorus.

Sometimes she got up and wandered among Loretta's roses. June had come in all its splendor, with great pink blooms as large as saucers, lovely flushed peace roses, and the scarlet and gold piccadilly. Their petals gleamed with dew, fragrant with distilled sweetness.

After dinner, Mickey offered to help clean up, even though the letter begged her to find her own secret place. Loretta jostled her good-naturedly.

"Not tonight. Go read your letter before it burns a hole in your pocket."

Gratefully Mickey hurried up the stairs. Her open window welcomed the good, outdoor smell of growing things. Mickey climbed out, stepping onto the limb that led her to the tree's heart.

From long practice, she snuggled her back against the perfectly shaped seat and pulled out her letter.

Dear Mickey,

Thank you for your letter and your interest in my friend Jami. Jami stayed with me several years. He has since moved, and I've lost track of him. However, I did forward your letter to his last address.

Disappointment coupled with a wild elation rose inside Mickey. If only Jami himself had written; but at least he was alive. Perhaps he would get in touch with her—someday.

I'll write him again, she decided. *Surely his friend will forward it.*

It was good to have something exciting to think about; her days had been stretching endlessly, making her almost wish she were back in school. Joel and Tam were rushed with end-of-the-year activities. They still picked her up on Sundays, but Mickey longed for something more. Everytime she brushed one of Loretta's rosebuds against her nose, her thoughts drifted back to the queen's bouquet.

She still kept it on her dresser. Every morning the dried roses and baby's breath tickled her nose. Every night it was the last thing she looked at when she turned off the light.

Mickey stuck the letter in her pocket and climbed back inside her room. She trotted downstairs and into the garden where she snipped a long-stemmed rose and selected a fern frond from the clump growing by the back door. Back inside, she arranged them in a slender white vase, then stepped back to admire the arrangement.

Kent and Loretta's voices came in through the open doorway.

"It isn't right, Kent!" Loretta exclaimed. "He doesn't want to go. Not deep inside."

"You're making him into a weakling!" Kent roared. "He needs to do the things he's afraid of!"

"But in his own time, Kent. On his own!"

"It's just a silly fear he has, Loretta."

Loretta's voice was shrilled. "Here you go again," she cried, "always pushing, pushing, never content with who or what your sons are!"

"Just a minute, Loretta!"

"You pushed Jami away with your foolish expectations. Now you're doing it to Steve! He's afraid of heights. Afraid! And you're forcing him to go rock rappelling, because—because you think it will make a man of him!"

There was a sudden silence. Mickey swallowed hard and made herself walk into the living room. A door slammed. Kent was gone.

Loretta sat alone on the couch, staring into space. She didn't even look up.

Mickey went over and timidly touched her shoulder.

"He's taking Steve rock rappelling at Smith Rock tomorrow," Loretta said dully. "I don't want them to go."

"It's good for fathers and sons to go off together sometimes," Mickey ventured.

"I—I know. But Steve's terribly afraid of heights."

"Perhaps if he faced up to it. You told me once I shouldn't always be running away."

Loretta smiled, an empty smile that didn't come from her heart. She sighed audibly. "But this is different—a phobia over which he has no control."

Mickey looked down at the rose still clutched in her hand. She held it out. "It's for you, Loretta."

Loretta took the white vase. "Um, lovely. You have a flair for things like this." She stood up. "Thank you, my dear. And don't fret about Kent and Steve. They'll do what they think is right."

She went away, and Mickey went in search of Steve.

She found him in the basement curled up with a book.

"Hi!" she said brightly. "Care if I join you?"

Steve's blue gaze was clouded with gray and was anything but welcoming. "Suit yourself," he grunted. He turned a page and went on reading.

"I hear you're going rock rappelling in the morning. Where at?"

"Smith Rock."

"Where's that?"

"Prineville area."

"Excited?"

Steve put his book down and glared at her. "You don't have to stay down here," he said coldly.

Mickey was undaunted. "I want to," she said. "I'm tired of being alone all day, and I need someone to talk to."

"Go talk to the robins."

"I already have. I need a person."

"Well," he said with exaggerated courtesy, "what shall we talk about?"

"Rock rappelling. Are you afraid, Steve?"

Steve moved his taut shoulders restlessly. "Of course not."

Mickey cocked her head to one side. "But I think you are."

She now had his complete attention. His eyes seemed more gray than blue as they bore into hers. "What makes you think so?"

"I heard your mom say you were afraid of heights. Have you always been?"

Steve took a deep breath. "Ever since I can remember, they've bothered me. Even going over some bridges makes me feel queer inside. And you've never seen Smith Rock. It goes almost straight up."

"Why does your dad want you to?"

"Because *he's* afraid!" he said scornfully.

"Your dad?"

"He's afraid I'll turn out like Jami. Run off, never amount to anything—" He turned his face away. "And I'm afraid too, afraid he'll never ever think I'm anybody worthwhile."

He jumped to his feet. "I'm climbing that rock, Mickey. I have to—"

I'm climbing that rock. I have to. I have to, echoed in Mickey's thoughts. "In a way he's running away, too," she muttered. "Away from the person he was meant to be."

She went up the stairs, through the living room, and on to her own aerie. Her Bible lay beside her bed.

She slipped to her knees. "I wish I knew how to pray," she whispered.

That night Mickey dreamed. A huge rock as big as a house teetered on a bluff. Her two brothers, just as she remembered them, played contentedly at its base.

A great fear overwhelmed her as the rock started to move. She must get to them!

"Mickey! Mickey!" Kevin screamed. There was a crash, then total blackness. Mickey jerked up in bed, her heart pounding.

"Kevin," she whispered. "Oh, Kevin. Are you all right?"

The darkness mocked her. She turned on the light and peered at the clock—five minutes past twelve. The urgency of the dream haunted her. She pulled on her robe and crept down the stairs.

Kent sat alone in the living room, the TV turned low. He held up his hand, silencing her, intent on hearing every word.

Feeling even more alone, Mickey slipped into the kitchen. Perhaps a cup of hot chocolate would send the dream horror from her.

She shivered as she waited for the water to boil, then turned. Kent stood in the doorway.

He scowled. "What are you doing up?" he demanded. "Aren't you happy here either?"

"Why—I—I just couldn't sleep. I had a dream—a rock. It was falling—"

"You too?" he roared. "Is everyone in this family against me?"

Mickey stared at him, unable to comprehend. "You mean Steve?" she blurted.

"You're two of a kind!" he blasted. "You're both afraid of your own shadows. Only with you it's your past. You've let it put chains around you. And what's it getting you? Nothing!"

Mickey's lips parted. She opened her mouth to say something—anything—but no words came. She ran past him, up the stairs and into her room. Tears of frustration burned her eyes.

She tossed her robe onto the pillow and began to dress in jeans, warm socks, and hooded sweatshirt. Then she went out the window and down the tree. She lit on the ground and ran.

Peter Rabbit, if she could just talk to Peter Rabbit. He'd been her special friend since the day she'd confided her heart to him about her mother. Kent and Loretta had said she should go back to see her, but Peter Rabbit never did. Somehow she felt he understood the turmoil inside her.

She stood outside his door, knocking nervously. No answer. She went to the window and tapped lightly. Still no response.

After a while she plodded back to the road, setting off slowly, then stepping faster away from Kent, away from Peter Rabbit, away from Loretta. Once her breath caught on something that sounded almost like a sob, but she kept on.

She stopped at the top of the hill, where Loretta had once waylaid her, now resting for a bit in the little shed where the children waited for the school bus, watching the big dipper dip low over a distant farmhouse. It almost seemed to be pouring.

Then she resumed her hike, her fingers jingling the change she'd stuffed into her pockets at the last minute. Slowly the night sky wheeled above her. But on she walked.

Toward morning, weariness overtook her. She saw a barn close by the road and crept inside. She curled up inside an untwined bale of hay beside the cows' stalls, numbly turning until she had a prickly nest.

"Jesus slept in a barn His first night on earth," she mused. Feeling strangely comforted, she fell asleep.

She wakened with a large black and white dog barking over her. Quickly she sat up, putting out a friendly hand. "Here, doggie, nice doggie, sh-h, doggie."

The dog stopped barking and stood still, his long tail hanging foolishly between his legs. His wet tongue lapped at her face. "No doggie, no—no—"

Slowly she got to her feet. Her fingers felt like ice, and she thought longingly of the hot chocolate she'd left behind.

But there was no help for it. "Maybe I'll go to Spring Valley in California," she said conversationally to her ardent admirer. "Paul Larson took Jami in. Maybe he'd take me, too." She stopped. Deep inside she knew she really wanted to go back to the Middletons.

"He's always yelling though. Well, not all the time, but—he's really a very miserable man.

"My mother said she couldn't stand yelling either. But I hate to think that I'm like her. Am I, dog?"

The canine's entire body began to accompany his wagging tail. A smile eased across Mickey's troubled face. She threw both arms around his great black and white neck. "Oh, dog," she whispered, "oh, dog."

After a while she started down the road. It was hard to make the dog realize he couldn't follow. "Home!" Mickey shouted. "Home! Home!" It hurt to have to pick up loose rocks from the side of the road with which to pelt him, but she did. At last he turned and left her, his tail between his legs, his shoulders hunched.

Mickey's tears almost began again. Would she always be hurting those who cared for her?

The sun rose high, and still she walked. Cars were beginning to move on the road. Several times she took shortcuts through small woodlands and fields.

One of them was a strawberry field. Mickey bent down and pushed the leaves back. A gleaming red strawberry, wet with dew, rewarded her.

"Um," she murmured, popping it into her mouth.

More followed. After she'd eaten her fill she continued on her way.

Estacada was much more distant than she realized. The road seemed endless, each curve hiding a longer stretch than she'd remembered. Her thighs began to tremble.

Even the town she'd once called "small" went on and on. She plodded from one street to the next until she finally reached a sign proclaiming, "Bus Stop." She peered up at it anxiously.

A woman, passing by, paused. "Bus service on Sunday is lousy," she said. "It'll be a good hour before one shows up."

Mickey thanked her as she moved away. Now what? Her stomach growled, making her keenly aware of her hunger. Never had a cup of chocolate sounded more tempting. Those lovely strawberries she'd consumed on the way to town seemed far away.

She walked down the street, searching for a cafe. A small white building advertising: AL'S COUNTRY COOKIN'—breakfast, lunches, dinners—reasonable prices, lured her.

She clutched her coins and moved closer. Through the window she saw the heads of diners. Her mouth watered.

Then she saw him, or was it? His back was to her, but she was sure she recognized his broad shoulders hunched forward, his brilliant curly hair—Joel.

Her heart clumped hard, her hand gripped the doorknob uncertainly. Should she go up to him or . . .

She pushed hard on the door. The noisy clatter of plates and silverware welcomed her. The fragrance of coffee and bacon permeated the air.

She slid into the chair beside him. He looked at her, then without a word beckoned to the waitress. "Hash browns, bacon and eggs, coffee."

The waitress slid a steaming cup in front of her. "I don't like coffee," Mickey whispered.

"Hot chocolate then," Joel said, "and put in plenty of whipped cream."

"I already had breakfast," Mickey protested feebly. "I ate strawberries, and I'd have had milk if I could have figured out how to get it out of the cow."

A smile slid across Joel's serious face. "Well," he drawled, "I think we can do better than that."

Mickey's throat thickened suddenly. "Why are you here? I thought you'd be in church."

Joel shook his head. "Not when a terrified Loretta calls me at three a.m. and asks if I had any idea where you might be—"

"Oh, no," Mickey whispered, "I'm sorry—"

"Then Kent talked to me. He was beside himself with worry. 'We've got to find her. We must—' So I put on my clothes, and I've been searching ever since." He made a sweeping gesture that took in the cafe. "This was my last idea of where you might show up."

The waitress brought her hot chocolate, and Mickey sipped it slowly, its warmth dissolving a bit of the tightness around her heart.

"Did they think I was running away again?" she asked.

Joel nodded. "I've never seen them so worried. They really love you, Mickey. Did you really mean to just up and walk out of their lives?"

"I—I don't know. I had this terrible dream. Then Kent misunderstood and thought I was accusing him of something—" She shook her head.

Joel touched her arm. "What's really bothering you, Mickey. Aren't you happy?"

"Sometimes I'm not," she whispered. "Sometimes I have this terrible longing, this awful yearning for—a place to call home. But I can never find it."

The waitress brought their hot food. "Oh," Mickey murmured. "I've never been so hungry."

Joel grabbed her hand, then bowed his head. "Thank you, Lord, for bringing Mickey here to me. And thank you for this food." He squeezed her hand quickly and released it. A pleasant sensation stirred inside Mickey.

She took a big bite of her hash browns. "They're perfect, Joel. So good—"

But Joel's mind wasn't on his food. "Did you read the book of John, Mickey?"

She nodded. "Yes. Then I started Luke."

"Good. I read something in Matthew yesterday that made me think of you."

Mickey stopped in the middle of a bite. "Me?"

"This man wanted to follow Jesus, but Jesus told him something that really hit me. He said, 'Foxes have holes, and birds of the air have nests, but the Son of Man has no where to lay His head!'"

"Jesus said that about himself?"

Joel nodded and picked up his toast. "He didn't have a place to call home either, Mickey. Not really."

"Not even when He was born?" Mickey murmured. Wonderment tinged her voice. "He must understand how I feel sometimes."

"He does, Mickey. Can't you imagine Him sleeping out on the desert, no pillow and no one who really understood him?"

"But He had His God," Mickey protested.

Joel nodded. "Yes, He had His Father. Because He did, He had everything He needed."

Mickey leaped to her feet, consternation on her face. "I need to call Loretta, tell her where I am."

" 'Atta girl, that you do. The telephone is back there."

When Mickey returned her face shone. "I talked to all of them!" she exclaimed. "Loretta said Kent had just come in to see if she'd heard anything when the phone rang. He's coming to get me right away—Loretta too!"

"Steve?"

"He said he was glad I was coming back. Then he said something kind of funny before he hung up." Bewilderment clouded her eyes. "He said, 'Thanks, big sister.' "

It was only after she was safe at home, alone in her own room, that she understood Steve's words. Her running off had kept Kent and Steve from ascending Smith Rock!

She ran her fingers over the soaring eagle poised on top of the totem pole. "Well, old eagle friend, you can soar over rocks, but my Steve can't. And you have a nest, too." She looked at her pillow. "And I—I too have a place to put my head. But Jesus . . ."

Twelve / Peter Rabbit Remembers

Mickey lay in bed, the darkness pressing around her. "Jesus, the Son of God, the Creator of the universe, with no place to lay His head . . ."

What would it be like to sleep on the ground? she wondered. She turned restlessly. *What was it Joel had said right before Kent had come for her?*

Ah, yes—"There's something really neat about Jesus, Mickey. Even though He didn't have any place to lay His head, He taught that anyone who comes to Him can have their own special place—in His heart. He's the Good Shepherd who loves and cares for each of His own."

A great longing filled her heart. She wished she could be one of Jesus' own.

She slipped out of bed and padded to the window. The cherry leaves rustled invitingly, giving her glimpses of winking stars. The moonlight, shattered by leaves, flooded the lawn.

Mickey went back to her bed and picked up the Indian blanket. Quietly, she stole down the stairs.

The ground beneath the cherry tree was hard and

lumpy. She thought about going back for her pillow, then decided against it. Jesus hadn't had any place to lay His head. . . .

She tilted her head back and let the majesty of the stars fill her. With them came a sense of wonder: The Creator of those great blinking worlds—the great God himself—a tiny baby; His mother wrapped Him gently and placed Him into a rough hay-filled manger.

Sudden tears filled her eyes. "Jesus," she said, "Mr. Hoffman says you're real, that I can talk to you. I'm not a good person, Jesus. I need you to forgive me, to live in me. I need a new life. . . ."

A new life, a new start, a new family. Mickey could sleep now. The hard ground cradled her, and the Creator of the universe put His great loving arms around her and gathered His new child close to His heart.

Mickey wakened suddenly. The dew on the grass was wet on her fingertips. For a moment she couldn't figure out where she was.

She turned her head and saw Kent's big boots pressing into the grass. She looked up. A worried frown creased his forehead.

"You scared me to death, Mickey," he said, his voice harsh with concern. "I thought you'd run off again."

Mickey struggled to a sitting position, the blanket wrapped tightly around her. It felt a little odd, almost like a cocoon.

The sun wasn't up yet, the pink streamers hung over the tops of the trees. Bird songs filled the air, not quite as lusty as April and May songs, but a joyous sound just the same.

She brushed her dark hair out of her eyes and smiled at Kent. "I'm sorry," she said. "I didn't mean to frighten you."

Kent squatted beside her. "What made you come out here?" he asked.

Mickey squinted thoughtfully. "I kept thinking about—about God—His greatness and majesty. And then how He left heaven and came to earth—a tiny baby—no place for Him there. It made me want to come out and look at the stars."

Kent was silent, his dark blue eyes fixed on the distant trees, the roaring creek. At last he spoke. "You think deep thoughts, Mickey. You're a good kid." He stood up. "What would you like for breakfast, Mickey girl?"

Mickey grinned. "French toast," she said, "and I'm going to fix it!"

She leaped to her feet, still swathed in her blanket. They raced together for the door.

After breakfast, Mickey sat for a long time in the living room. Both Kent and Loretta had hurried off to work and Steve to school. The day stretched long and unbroken before her.

A great longing rose inside her. She wanted to tell Joel and Tam about her decision in the night. Instead, she went upstairs, drawing her letter from Paul Larson out of the totem pole where she'd hidden it.

That afternoon she wrote a long letter to Jami and put it into the mailbox. Perhaps if he knew that God was a God of new beginnings . . .

When she came in, she telephoned Tam. Tam answered right away, her voice eager.

"Ah," she teased, "Mickey, the gal who comes to church just so she can date my good-looking brother . . . Mickey, are you there?"

Slowly Mickey put down the receiver. "I can't tell her about last night," she whispered. "She'll think I did it to get Joel."

Another thought, even more terrible, plunged through her. *Joel will think that, too . . .*

She turned and ran from the room, the telephone shrilling behind her. She flew across the lawn, past the bridge, then climbed high up on the bluff overlooking the stream and hatchery.

Jim was down there. She saw his head silhouetted dark against the cement background.

After a while she joined him beside the runway that held the smaller fish. He smiled at her, his nose twitching in the way she'd come to love. "Troubled again, Little Bunny?"

Mickey nodded. She sat down on the ledge and stared at him. "Peter Rabbit, do you have many friends?"

Jim's nose twitched again. He cocked his eyebrows into a question as he sat down beside her. "Why do you ask, Mickey?"

"Because today I tried to share something special with a friend. But she—she—"

"Misunderstood? Friends do that sometimes, you know. Don't take it too hard."

"But it was something so very special. And I thought it would make her happy!"

"Want to tell me, Little Bunny?"

"Yes. You know how alone I've always felt, so out of things somehow?"

Jim nodded. "No place to call home."

"Right. Well, I've discovered something new." Mickey struggled for words. "It's something about a person—the Lord Jesus Christ."

"Go on."

"He didn't have any place to lay His head either. He even said the birds have nests and the foxes holes to sleep in, but He didn't have any place.

"Remember once how you told me you had a special place a long time ago when you were a boy? Jesus didn't even have that."

Jim's dark eyes grew dreamy, reminiscent. "It was just outside my bedroom window. I'd crawl out, and there I'd be, looking down, way down. I could see the water flashing, the top of the grape arbor, the baby birches. Sometimes my mother would be out in the garden kneeling among the carrots and tomatoes, her dark hair so smooth and shining. My baby brother toddling beside her—"

Mickey took a sharp breath inward. She stared at him. He frowned at her, the faraway look dissolving from his eyes. "Why are you looking at me like that?"

"Why—why—it's nothing," she mumbled.

"Now—what were you saying before I went off on my childhood tangent?"

"Just that—that—Jesus is my special friend now. We're together somehow."

Jim stood up. He reached out and touseled her soft dark hair. "I'm glad, Little Bunny. Everyone needs a friend they can count on. I'm going home now. Don't forget, I'm your friend too."

After he left, Mickey still sat there. Tam's teasing words still bothered her.

Would everyone at church think she'd decided for Jesus just to get Joel? Mickey pushed her troubled thoughts aside. Jim's reminiscences were more important . . .

After dinner, Mickey climbed out her window and settled herself among the branches. She looked down— down—

She saw the flashing stream, the tops of the birch trees, Steve's brown hair . . .

Eagerly she hurried to join him. He was standing alone on the bank watching the great gray fish lying at the bottom of the creek.

He smiled at her. "They're so beautiful, aren't they—so still, so quiet. I wonder what their world is like?"

"Different than ours," Mickey changed the subject abruptly. "Did your family once have grapes here—and space for a garden?"

"How did you know?" he asked curiously.

"I didn't—I just wondered."

Steve gestured toward the lawn. "We used to grow grapes there, along the edge. We took them out several years ago because they never produced well. And down in the low space, below where those tiny trees are growing—that used to be Mother's garden."

Mickey nodded slowly. "Do you remember it much?"

"A little bit. Once I pulled out a whole bunch of carrots trying to help weed. I was real little then." He looked suddenly wistful. "I sort of miss it, in a way. But now that Mother works so much at the pharmacy, well, she can't do everything."

Mickey agreed, then went in search of Loretta. She found her kneeling among her roses, a sharp trowel in her hand, a can of rose food beside her. She leaned back on her heels and smiled at Mickey.

"Do you have any old photo albums, Loretta? I'd like to see what everyone used to look like." She made a sweeping gesture. "And the house and the grounds."

Loretta got to her feet, wiping her hands on her stained blue jeans. She laid her trowel on the path and went inside.

Mickey followed her into her bedroom. She seldom went in there, but now she wanted an excuse to look at Margot's picture. Would there be a resemblance to Peter Rabbit?

Loretta opened a drawer and pulled out several albums. Mickey looked at Margot. Her dark brown eyes, her dimpling smile, all spoke of a much loved, spoiled young girl. Mickey frowned, but she could see no resemblance to Peter Rabbit except for the shape of her large brown eyes.

"Did Jami look like Margot?" she asked.

Loretta looked up. "Why—no—not especially. They were both dark though, nice looking with those big eyes. Only Jami's were like his father's, dark blue. Margot's were brown."

"She has dimples around her mouth when she smiles like that," Mickey observed.

"So did Jami. I used to love it when he'd smile that

teasing, half-laughing grin of his."

She handed several albums to Mickey. "Let's take them into the kitchen."

Together they spread the albums on the table. "Here's one of Steve when he was only two."

A frowning baby in a wheelbarrow scowled up at her.

"He was miserable that day," Loretta remembered. She turned the page. "Here's one of Kent and Jami."

Excitement poured into Mickey as she bent over it. Kent and Jami stood facing the camera, smiling broadly. A hat was pulled low over Jami's eyes, but she didn't miss his dimples lurking at the corners of his mouth. He was tall, like Peter Rabbit, but not as broad.

"That was taken a few months before he left," Loretta explained. She glanced at the clock. "Goodness, it's 7:30 already, and I told Louise I'd be there by eight. You can put the albums on my bed when you finish looking." She hurried away.

Mickey turned the pages slowly: Steve dangling his first fish in the air; Kent's silhouette against the bank; Loretta stirring something over a camp stove; Margot dressed in a frilly, white dress.

Loretta popped back into the kitchen. She picked up an old, navy blue album from the bottom of the stack, explaining, "I almost forgot. This is one I never let out of my sight."

Mickey stared after her, a faint question forming in her mind. *Was there something in that old album that Loretta didn't want her to see? Didn't want her to find out about?*

But no, she was growing silly, fanciful. The phone

rang and Mickey hurried to answer it.

It was Tam. She came straight to the point. "I'm sorry, Mickey. I was only teasing when I said you were coming to church just so Joel would date you. I didn't mean it—not really."

"Then you shouldn't have said it," Mickey said tartly.

"I know. It was mean of me—really. Can you forgive me?"

Mickey took a deep breath. "Is that what Joel thinks, too?" she asked.

"Of course not. You know how boys are. Even if they thought it, they wouldn't say it!"

"Did you tell it to Joel?"

"Look, Mickey. It was my own silly idea. I—"

"Did you tell Joel what you thought?" Mickey persisted.

"Well—not exactly. But he doesn't think it, Mickey. Really he doesn't. Does it matter so much?"

"Yes, it does. I wish you hadn't, Tam."

"Oh, come on. I'm not perfect. We're still friends, aren't we?"

"I suppose," Mickey said wearily. "But next Sunday you don't need to come for me. I have someone else to take me to church."

As she put the receiver down, Mickey wondered who it might be.

Thirteen / Steve Catches a Poacher

Tam's teasing remark that so upset Mickey didn't keep Joel away after all. Saturday afternoon Mickey heard his voice at the front door asking for her.

She flew out of the kitchen. Joel stood on the porch, brushing his shoes against the mat in front of the door, a small, light-blue backpack perched high on his shoulders.

"Hi," he greeted. "I've got some hamburger. Want to go make a fire and help cook it?"

Mickey's face brightened. "I've never done it," she said uncertainly.

"I've got matches and a fry pan. Got any hot chocolate mix?"

"I'll see." She hurried back into the kitchen. "Loretta, do we have any chocolate that I could take picnicking? That is, if you don't mind—"

In a few minutes she reappeared, her cheeks flushed with enthusiasm. "I've got chocolate mix, salt and pepper and some buns." She held them out triumphantly.

"Good girl." He slung his pack from his shoulder

and began pushing her contribution inside.

"Where are you going to picnic?" Loretta asked.

"I thought at that little grill above the whale hole. You know, the place we swim."

"But not today—"

Joel glanced through the window at the sunshine tracing leaf patterns on the lawn. "The sun's warm," he said, "but the water's too cold in June. Come July—"

They set out along the service road behind the hatchery. Mickey took a deep breath, delighting in the stream rushing over mossy rocks, glinting golden-green in the sunshine.

"Someday I'd like to hike far enough to discover the stream's source," she said.

Joel smiled. "Me too." He glanced at her curiously. "You seem different today, Mickey. Happier."

Mickey's chin jerked. "I—"

Joel stopped. "Come on. Tell me."

A flush rose high in Mickey's cheeks. "I wanted to—but Tam—"

A quizzical smile lurked at the corners of Joel's lips. "Okay. What's my ever-lovin' sister been up to this time?"

"Nothing really," Mickey stammered. She tried to change the subject. "Come on. I'm starved."

Joel reached out and held her arm. "It must be something good—or you wouldn't look so happy. Come on," he entreated, "tell me."

Mickey lowered her eyes and started walking. "I asked Jesus into my life Monday night," she whispered.

She looked up, unprepared for the joy that leaped into Joel's eyes. His hand tightened on her arm. "But you wanted me to be the first to know!" he cried. "That's wonderful—wonderful!"

"I know. It's just that I thought people would say I'd done it just so you would date me."

"That's nonsense," Joel sputtered, "utter nonsense—Where did you get such an idea?"

"But Tam said—"

"What?"

"Right after I met you she said you were funny, that she thought you liked me but that you wouldn't date me unless—unless I was a Christian." She bit her lip. "She said something on the telephone that made me think she thought that was the reason I was going to church."

Joel frowned. "Is it?"

"At first it was, just a little bit," Mickey explained bravely. "But after I'd gone a few times, I wanted to keep going no matter what."

Joel looked thoughtful. "Tam said something to me, too. She started teasing me about lowering my standards by dating a girl who wasn't a Christian. Funny, I hadn't even thought of our hiking along the creek, going to the May Day festivities as dates."

He caught her hand and grinned broadly. "Well, how about it? Want to go on a date? A real one?"

Mickey stopped dead in her tracks. "Do you mean it?"

"Yes, I do."

Mickey looked at him. There was a serious intent in his green eyes. This was no joke.

"I'd like to take you somewhere special," he continued, "partly to celebrate your decision for Christ and partly—because you're a very, very special girl."

A smile lit his entire face. He caught his lower lip between his teeth. "If you could choose a place to go, Mickey, where would it be?"

Mickey clasped her hands in front of her. "I'd like to dress up special and go to dinner—on the River Queen. Except—that's rather expensive."

Joel shook his head. "Doesn't matter. In a few days I'll be helping roof the house Dad's working on. Besides, he already told me he'd finance a school's-out splurge." He spread his arms wide. "Fringe benefit, you understand. Let's plan it for Tuesday evening. I'll pick you up about five—"

"I'll ask Kent and Loretta."

"And so will I! In the meantime, where's supper?"

They laughed joyously and headed up the hill in high spirits. On one side of them the creek flashed and leaped; on the other, vine maple, ferns and moss hung over their heads, transforming the high bank into a forest wonderland.

The road meandered farther up the hill, leaving the stream behind. But Joel and Mickey detoured into a sun-drenched grassy meadow, complete with a small grill. Joel slung his backpack beside it and joined Mickey on the high bank overlooking the creek.

A narrow path veered down to the edge where a large rock jutted far out into the stream, forming a smooth, gray peninsula that reared upward into the air.

"Is that the whale?" Mickey asked.

Joel nodded. "It's the only spot along here that's deep enough to swim in in the summertime. It's fun to dive off the whale."

"This must be the place where the Middletons lost

their daughter," she observed, noting the water swirling around the whale's head. "It looks safe enough. Maybe she misjudged and dived too wide—hit the shallows. I understand she was a strong swimmer."

A slight frown clouded Joel's eyes. "I'd almost forgotten." He looked at her. "Did you ever get an answer from the letters you sent to Spring Valley?"

"Yes. Paul Larson wrote. He said he'd lost contact with Jami but was forwarding my letter to Jami's last address. Later I wrote Jami another letter telling him about my beginning a new life in Christ." She picked up a fallen stick and absently began pulling at the tiny fringes of dead moss.

"Something else happened, too, Joel. Peter Rabbit—I mean Jim—" She twisted a fragment of dead bark from her stick and tossed it into the stream. "He said something that made me think he might be the Middletons' missing Jami."

"But that's impossible, Mickey," Joel protested. "How could he be, so close and all, and Kent and Loretta not knowing?"

"I looked at Jami's picture in their album," she insisted. "Jim *could* be him. He'd be nine years older now—bigger—heavier, and his black beard would make him look different." She giggled. "I'd like to shave it off and see if he has dimples at the corners of his mouth."

"But surely when they came face to face they'd know."

"Probably. But yesterday Loretta was looking out the window when Jim walked by the road. She wanted to know who it was, and I explained it was my friend Jim. Then she sighed and said, 'Isn't it awful to have neighbors so close and not even know them?' "

Joel looked at her curiously. "What was it Jim said that made you think—"

"He was remembering—from his childhood. But of course, I could be mistaken." She shrugged. "Where do we get the water for hot chocolate?"

Joel unzipped his pack and pulled out an old battered coffeepot.

"From the creek. It's purer than most city water." He hurried down the tiny trail to the water's edge.

Mickey busied herself with supper preparations, steadying the fry pan on a rock close to the grill, slitting open a package of cookies, crumbly with cinnamon and sugar.

"We forgot spoons, Joel!"

"We can use my knife."

"Or little sticks."

They scrambled through the underbrush in search of fallen branches for kindling. They returned triumphant, their arms filled with dead wood.

Kneeling on one knee, Joel touched a lighted match to the dry fir needles. The flame caught, burning brightly.

"I could eat that hamburger raw," Joel grumbled.

The margarine under the patties sizzled; the buns toasted a light golden brown; steam rose from the coffeepot spout.

They sat with their backs braced against the smooth shoulder of a rock and ate their juicy burgers. They were caught away in their own little world of warm sunshine, green grass and the laughing creek.

When the sun withdrew from their sheltered nook,

they stuffed the picnic remains into the pack and doused the fire. Reluctant to have their day end, they walked back slowly.

Instead of turning toward the pink house, they crossed the bridge below the hatchery and followed the stream downward.

Joel pushed a sagging branch aside. He nodded at the place the deer had been wedged beneath the water. "Remember Morning?"

Mickey smiled. *Morning, the spirit of the creek—her tiny carving, the totem pole, Jami . . .*

The sun was gone. No longer did the forest shadows beckon and allure. But still Joel and Mickey lingered, wandering farther and farther downstream. Joel stopped suddenly, his finger on his lips.

Mickey peered around his broad shoulders; Steve was crouched behind a log, staring intently at something just beyond their gaze.

Joel moved forward cautiously, and Mickey followed. A twig snapped beneath her foot. Steve's head jerked, turning toward them.

Curiosity rose inside Mickey as she noticed a camera clutched tightly in his hand. She opened her mouth to ask a question, then stifled it as he shook his head and made a wild pointing gesture downstream.

Two men on the bank below him were cutting open the bellies of two fish. Even in the dusk Mickey saw the blood on their hands, the rosy eggs tumbling into their bucket.

Steve gestured to Joel and Mickey to turn back. His mouth soundlessly articulated. "Police."

Joel grabbed her hand. They bent low, slinking furtively beneath the bushes. When they were out of sight, they broke into a run.

"Telephone—" Joel gasped. "Your house—"

They headed for it, legs flying, hair blowing. Mickey burst through the door. The telephone was in her hand. *This has happened before*, she thought. But this time there was no dial tone. Her fingers pushed the buttons down—once—twice, no buzz, nothing. "It's dead!" she cried.

Joel grabbed the receiver from her and put it to his ear. "You're right! The hatchery—"

"No! Jim's house is closer."

They rushed out the door, down the road, across the grass and onto Jim's porch. But there was no answer to Joel's wild knocking. Mickey pushed past him and shoved open the door. A telephone was on a small desk, close by. Mickey picked up the receiver and handed it to Joel.

He dialed rapidly as Mickey gasped for breath. Her fingers nervously pushed back her hair, then toyed with the paperweight beside the phone.

"Police? We've got a poaching problem on Eagle Creek. Right below the hatchery."

Joel replaced the receiver and turned to her. "They'll have a car here in a few minutes. I'm going to the bridge to meet them."

He touched her shoulder gently. "You stay here. Explain to Jim." Then he was gone, hurrying out the door.

Mickey took a great sobbing breath and closed her eyes for a moment. When she opened them she was staring at a miniature totem pole clutched tightly in her hands. Awe held her as she touched the graceful deer, the trout, the soaring eagle.

She lifted her head, observing the room's details: the comfortable couch against the wall, covered with a colorful Indian blanket, a painting of a water ouzel darting beneath a waterfall, green drapes tied back to let in the outdoors . . .

The back door opened and closed softly. There was the sound of footsteps. Quickly she put the totem pole paperweight back on its pile of envelopes, but not before she saw—her letter—addressed to Jami.

She whirled around. Peter Rabbit looked solemnly at her.

Fourteen / The Prodigal Son

Jim and wildly excited Mickey joined Steve, Joel and the officer at the patrol car parked on the bridge. Steve's blue eyes snapped. He flashed Mickey a wide grin.

A strong satisfaction tingled deep inside her. *Catching those poachers will be good for Steve*, she thought. She forgot the awful moment when Jim had come in and found her staring at the papers on his desk—when his mouth still smiled, but a shutter had closed her out of his eyes.

"This is my sister, Mickey," Steve was saying. "And Jim from the hatchery."

"Glad to meet you." The officer laid the completed papers inside the open car. "Your brother was the instigator of a fine bit of action," he told Mickey. "He not only had this young man call us quickly, he also recorded the evidence with his pocket camera."

Joel grasped Steve's shoulder proudly. "No panic— just quick thinking. A great job."

"It was done in such a systematic fashion that it surprised me," the officer agreed. He slid behind the wheel, closing the door behind him. "Many thanks!" he called.

The car was scarcely out of sight when Steve tossed his camera wildly into the air. "Yippee!" he yelled. "Yippee!" He caught it and ran toward home.

Jim turned to Mickey. "Proud of your brother?" he asked.

Hope flared inside her. Had her intrusion been forgiven? She nodded. *And I'm proud of you, too,* she wanted to cry. *You came back when you could have stayed away—forever.*

Instead she held out her hand. "I'm sorry about busting in like we did."

Jim smiled. His expression reminded Mickey of a person caught between the present and a memory.

He took Mickey's hand. "It's all right," his lips said. But his eyes, which had reminded Mickey of deep, understanding wells, were still veiled.

Mickey felt her eyes burn. "Good night," she whispered.

Joel and Mickey watched him walk away across the hatchery grounds.

"A man with a past," she murmured. "I wonder . . ."

Joel caught her hand. "Let's go to your house. I want to be in on the excitement when Steve tells Kent and Loretta."

They hurried home. Loretta had apparently just returned; her sweater and purse were carelessly thrown on the table. She sat forward on her chair, her gray eyes glowing as Steve regaled her with his tale.

"Why, Steve," she marveled over and over.

"You should have seen their faces when I handed the cop the film from my camera," he boasted. "He said—"

"He was loud in his praise of Steve," Joel interrupted. "He said he couldn't believe that one so young could organize such an orderly plan of action."

Loretta shone, her excitement and pride plainly equaling Steve's. "I can hardly wait to tell Kent," she whispered in an aside to Mickey.

Goose bumps erupted on Mickey's arms. "Me either," she whispered, giving Loretta a hug.

"I wonder what's wrong with that telephone," Joel wondered, suddenly remembering.

The boys examined it. "The plug's out of the jack!" Joel exclaimed sheepishly. He looked at Mickey, and they burst out laughing.

After they calmed down, Joel left. But the excited family waited, eager to share with Kent their pride in Steve's adventure. Loretta popped a huge bowl of popcorn and put it in the middle of the table. In the midst of their munching, a car roared down the hill. Kent!

Kent looked at them curiously as he pushed open the door. "What's up?" he asked.

"Steve has something to tell, Kent!" Loretta cried, "something important!"

The popcorn was forgotten as Mickey watched wonder and pride grow on Kent's dark, rugged face. "Why, son," he murmured. "Why, son—"

After a while Mickey slipped out. Steve needed to be alone with his family in the hour of his triumph. And she—she needed to be alone too.

The flashing creek, the sizzling meat, the sunshine warm on the boulder flashed like a kaleidoscope through her thoughts. With them came Joel's voice. *"How about it? Will you date me?"* Then, *"Where to?" The River*

Queen . . .

Then another memory, tinged with confusion. Jim standing in the doorway. He'd only spoken two words, "Well, Mickey?"

Shame had enveloped her, shame for standing there looking at his papers. A flush had risen into her cheeks as she'd tried to explain . . . about the poachers, Steve, Joel, the telephone . . .

Quickly Mickey undressed. It wasn't until she was snuggled deep beneath her blanket that she remembered her words to Tam on that far-off Tuesday evening.

"Don't bother to pick me up Sunday. I already have a ride."

Mickey pushed the blankets back. Should she call Joel? She hesitated, stubborn pride restraining her.

Jim—would he? She knew she needed to talk to him, to break down the wall that had risen between them when he had seen her standing by his desk . . .

She tossed on her robe and hurried down the stairs. The living room was dark. She turned on the lights and picked up the telephone, a prayer rising from her heart. *Lord, help me.*

"Peter Rabbit?"

"Yes, Mickey. What is it?"

But words to break down the wall didn't come. Mickey swallowed hard. "Could you—do something for me? Like take me to church in the morning?"

There was a long silence. Then a sigh. "Well, I'm not much of a church-going man, Mickey. But for you—"

There was another long pause. Mickey felt her heart thudding against her ribs.

"For you, Little Bunny, I will. What time do we leave?"

Mickey went back upstairs—but not to sleep. After a while she opened her Bible to her favorite verses and began to read:

> As they were walking along the road, a man said to him, "I will follow you wherever you go."
> Jesus replied, "Foxes have holes and birds of the air have nests, but the Son of Man has no place to lay his head."
> He said to another man, "Follow me."

Mickey smiled. "Yes, Jesus," she whispered, "I'll follow you—anywhere—"

That night Mickey dreamed of a single mountain, still and white, stretching into the sky. A single trail wound around and around it, and that was all there was in the dream.

She wakened with thoughts of single things. A bright red strawberry, a drop of water, a solitary leaf, a lonely eagle rising into the sky. One God, one Savior, Mighty One.

She opened her eyes. The darkness had fled while she slept, and now the room was flooded with light. She watched a shaft of sunlight creep into the open closet door, slide down the sleeve of her white blouse, highlight her purple dress.

She got up and began pushing the hangers apart. She chose her soft pink-flowered dress and slid into it, feeling a tiny bit like a part of the morning. She held her hands out wide and whirled in a circle, wondering if Jim would be brave enough to come to the door for her.

She ran downstairs and into the kitchen—put bread into the toaster, raisin bran in her bowl. She poured milk on the cereal and sat down.

The doorbell rang while she was still eating. She shoved the bowl into the sink, grabbed her sweater and opened the door.

Jim stood there, resplendent in a navy blue suit and matching tie. His dark hair was in place, his beard neatly trimmed.

Mickey gasped. "I've never seen you dressed up before, Jim—"

Jim's lips managed a smile. His nose twitched nervously. "What happened to Peter Rabbit?" he asked.

Mickey quickly recovered her poise. "I think he went out the window with your old khaki pants!" Inside, her thoughts whispered, *or did I frighten him away when I burst uninvited into his hollow tree?*

She determinedly shoved her thoughts away and caught up her Bible from the couch. "You do look nice, Jim," she said, deliberately choosing to sidestep the difficulty between them. "Has Meredith ever seen you dressed up like that?"

Jim looked startled. "Who told you about Meredith?"

"Steve. He told me she was your girlfriend. Is she, Jim?"

Jim didn't answer. He strode on ahead and quietly opened the car door for her.

Mickey tried to cover her distress with a constant patter of conversation. Jim didn't seem to be listening. At last she stopped trying and just looked at the scenery.

June was the month of green, she decided. Green grass, green trees, green—green—green. Even the churchyard was filled with it: the bushes at the entrance, the carefully clipped hedge, the wide lawn.

Mickey stole a look at Jim's face. *He looks ill at ease*, she thought. *Perhaps I shouldn't have asked him to take me.*

A little lady in a powder blue dress hurried up to them. "Why, Mickey," she exclaimed, "you've brought your brother!"

Confusion rushed through Mickey. She glanced at Jim. A strange look covered his face like a curtain. *He's thinking of Margot*, Mickey thought, with a flash of insight.

"No," she said, smiling up at Jim. "But I wish he were."

Mr. Hoffman came over to them. Mickey introduced the two men, then watched as he guided Jim to the young adult class.

In Mickey's classroom, Joel slid into a chair next to hers.

"How did you get here?" he asked.

"Jim brought me," she whispered.

A scowl wrinkled Joel's forehead.

"Aren't you glad?" she faltered.

Joel raised his eyebrows, silencing her questioning. Across the room, Tam smiled at her. It was an uncertain smile tinged with regret. Something painful flashed through Mickey. *I need to forgive her.*

It was hard to concentrate on Mr. Hoffman's words that morning. Mickey's thoughts kept racing to the young adult class. *Would they intimidate shy Peter Rabbit with their eagerness and knowledge? Would he want to come again?*

Mickey slipped out of class as soon as Mr. Hoffman

dismissed them. She hurried to the foyer. Jim stood by a table, obviously looking for her.

She smiled and went over to him. "Shall we go inside?"

They found a place in the back pew, close by the door. A pang went through Mickey as she watched her own class members squeeze together into a pew close to the front. Joel was there, sitting close to auburn-headed Julie.

The music began. Mickey began to sing, carefully concentrating on the words the way Mr. Hoffman had suggested they do. Her spirit lifted. She was singing to her Lord! She was His child!

The Scripture passage that morning was from the book of Luke. Mickey caught her breath as the sweetness of the story of the lost son wrapped itself around her. She knew what it was to be lost and alone.

She glanced at Jim out of the corner of her eye. He listened intently, his eyes glued to the minister.

" 'And he arose, and came to his father. But when he was yet a great way off, his father saw him, and had compassion, and ran, and fell on his neck, and kissed him.' "

The minister laid his Bible on the pulpit and leaned forward. "Can any of us know, really know, the emotions that were going through that young man's heart— the heart of the father?

"This is the story Jesus told to illustrate to the tax collectors and sinners how much they were loved by their God. The son was far from home, no friends, nothing left that he could call his own. Yet his father loved him! He was watching, waiting, longing for him to come home. When he did, he ran to meet him. He hugged him, kissed him.

"What love! What perfect love! A love that's big enough to forgive. A love that's big enough to risk everything for someone else."

Mickey looked up at Jim's face. There were tears in his eyes. She was sure she saw them.

She reached over and timidly touched his hand. He squeezed hers, then released it. "I have to go, Mickey," he whispered. "I'm sorry—"

And he was gone. Mickey felt tears form in her own eyes. *Oh, Jami, come home, come home.*

For a moment she covered her face with her hands. "What is God saying to you right now?" the minister asked. "That there's someone you need to forgive? Someone in your past that you're holding apart from, maybe even waiting for them to take the first step."

Mickey heard no more. *Tam,* her heart cried. Then—*Mother—Mother.*

Fifteen / I'm Michelle Ann Strand

Tears blurred Mickey's eyes. The faces in the church foyer swam in a haze of colors.

Tam's long arms reached out, squeezing her shoulder. "I'm sorry," she whispered, "me and my big mouth—"

Mickey blinked hard. "I'm sorry too. After you called I didn't want to forgive you."

Tam leaned close. "Joel told me. We're sisters in Christ now."

"Sisters!" Mickey's eyes widened. She looked at the people surging around her, heard their eager greetings, their laughter. "My new family!" she gasped.

Tam laughed with obvious delight. Joel joined them, taking Tam's arm. "Where is Jim?" he asked Mickey.

"I—I don't know. I think the sermon got to him." She smiled a weak quavering smile. "I know it did me."

"Need a ride home?"

Mickey swallowed hard. "Please."

After they let Tam out at a friend's house, Mickey explained her reaction to the story of the prodigal son.

"For me it had to do with forgiveness," Mickey said. "Ever since my mother left me I've been tangled up inside. First I'd hate her. Then I'd love her. Then I'd start over again hating—feeling bitter, resentful."

"And now?" Joel prodded.

Mickey turned big, dark eyes toward him. He noted the smudges beneath them, the lashes still stuck together like a tired child's.

"Now, more than anything else, I want to forgive her," Mickey said in a low voice. "And I think—I think it's something I have to do now."

She clasped her hands tightly in front of her. "I think I have to accept her as she is—with all her faults and weaknesses," her voice broke, "just like Jesus accepted me."

She turned to face him. "When I saw her at the hospital, I hated her for what she did, who she was—a woman never satisfied, running from one man to another.

"But even more, she frightened me. Would I grow up to be like her? Afraid to face responsibility? Always running from difficulties? from pain?"

Joel turned off onto a side road. Eagle Fern Park closed in around them; great firs and lofty maples rose on each side like a cathedral.

They got out of the car and walked over to a picnic table. They sat down with their backs braced against the table and looked at each other.

"Choosing to forgive your mother is a step in the right direction, Mickey. But it's not humanly possible."

"I know. It's something I have to let Jesus do through me, isn't it?"

Joel nodded. "But since the Holy Spirit living inside

you brought it to your attention," he reached out, touching her hand, "then He'll give you the strength."

"What I'm afraid of is that I'll not say it right, Joel. Or that right in the middle, hate will overcome me again, and I'll make everything worse."

Joel sighed deeply. He looked up at the green canopy of leaves rustling over their heads. Mickey had the feeling he was praying.

A chipmunk, growing suddenly bold, darted onto the edge of the table. Joel lowered his gaze, and the visitor with the bright inquisitive eyes and the question mark tail dashed beneath the table.

Mickey smiled. "The little darling."

"Would it help if I went with you?" Joel asked. "I'd pray every minute, squeeze your hand if you even started to say something unkind."

Mickey caught her breath, biting her lower lip. "Would you really?"

"Yes, I would. I'd consider it a privilege."

"Then," Mickey said thoughtfully, "I think I'll say yes."

She jumped up. The chipmunk scurried out from under the table and flashed up the fir, his tail arched, his angry chatter echoing through the park.

They laughed. "Funny little visitor," Mickey said. "I wish I had something to give him."

"We'll come back later. Maybe for a picnic." Joel caught her hand. "When should we see your mother?"

"I'm not sure. I'll have to call Mrs. Morton, find out where Mother is now."

But getting her mother's address wasn't as easy as Mickey thought.

"I'm sorry, Mickey," Mrs. Morton told her. "I don't

have it. You could call the hospital. Maybe they'd give it to you."

But they wouldn't. "I'm sorry, but we don't give out that kind of information over the telephone. If you'd like to come in—talk to the supervisor."

Mickey put the receiver down in disgust, then called Joel. "There's just one thing to do, Mickey," he said. "We'll go to the hospital—together."

It was hard for Mickey to enter the busy reception room, harder still to be ushered into a tiny room and told to wait. Through the open door, the loudspeaker called, "Dr. Molaski, Dr. Molaski, please." Mickey clutched Joel's hand, a metallic taste rising in her throat.

A smiling woman in a black skirt and deep purple blouse hurried into the room. "I'm Mrs. McAllister, assistant administrator. May I help you?"

Mickey licked her lips. "It's about a patient who was here a month ago: Joanne Cochran. I'd like her address."

"Just a moment." Mrs. McAllister left the room, and came back carrying a folder. She leafed through it, her long, slim hands efficient. When she looked up, her quick gray glance was impersonal. "I'm sorry. She left specific instructions not to give it to anyone."

Mickey suddenly sat forward, squaring her shoulders. "But I'm not just anyone," she said. "I'm her daughter, Michelle Ann Strand. I have every right to know where she is."

The woman raised an eyebrow. She looked at Mickey intently, then turned toward the door. "Another minute—"

Joel put his arm around Mickey's shoulder. "Good

for you, Mickey," he whispered. His arm tightened. "Michelle Ann Strand." The way he rolled it on his tongue made it sound beautiful.

Tears stung Mickey's eyes and she blinked. She opened her purse and took out a tissue.

Mrs. McAllister came back with a piece of paper. She handed it to Mickey. "Your mother was discharged to this address ten days ago. Good luck."

Mickey thanked her, and she and Joel hurried to the car. "Do you think we can find it?" Mickey asked uncertainly. "It's on Northeast Hoyt Street."

Joel was unconcerned. "We've got all afternoon."

It almost took them that long to find it. They discovered dead-end streets, one-ways going the wrong way, detours for street repairs, and they also misread signs and took wrong turns.

At last a shabby gray house on a busy corner revealed the number the woman had given them. They parked on the street and ascended a narrow flight of steps along the outside of the house.

"This can't be it, can it?" Mickey muttered, observing the sagging rail, the dirty curtains covering the windows. The hard ache in her throat was back, worse than before. "Oh, Joel. What an awful place to come when you're sick—and down."

Joel knocked, but there was no answer. A vast emptiness seemed to echo at them. He knocked again, his forehead creasing into a scowl.

Mickey sat down on the steps. She looked up at Joel. "If I could write her a letter!"

Joel nodded and ran to the car. He hurried back, pressing a page of notebook paper into her hands.

Mickey took it, her fingers cold. She clutched the pencil. "But I don't know what to say!"

Joel joined her on the steps, his long legs stretching below hers. "Just follow your heart, Mickey. Follow your heart."

But the words wouldn't come. Desperately Mickey chewed on the pencil. Joel patted her shoulder and stood up. "I'll be back in a little while."

Mickey watched the car move away—noted Joel's encouraging smile, his quick wave. Then he was gone.

The rush of tears she'd been fighting for so long broke loose. Sitting alone on the gray, battered steps, Mickey wept—for her mother and her father, for all the happiness they might have had—and hadn't.

After a while, she mopped the tears away and began to write:

> Dear Mother,
>   I love you and want to say I'm sorry—for blaming you, for hating you.
>   The reason I can say it is because I have a new life now. It has to do with a person—the Lord Jesus Christ . . .

She pushed it under the door and ran down the steps. Joel's car drew close to the curb, and she hopped inside.

Joel patted a sack lying on the front seat. "We're going to picnic at the park with our chipmunk and— Colonel Sanders."

The smell of the fried chicken suddenly made Mickey's mouth water. She smiled. "Let's go," she agreed. "I'm hungry."

That night Mickey dreamed she was in a canyon,

surrounded by high, reddish bluffs. Peter Rabbit walked toward her. "So you're Michelle Ann Strand," he said, "Michelle Ann Strand."

His voice echoed off the canyon walls, "Michelle Ann Strand." "Michelle Ann Strand . . ."

Mickey wakened suddenly, the walls reverberating with her name. Terror filled her. It took her a moment to realize it was only a part of a dream.

She turned on the light. The walls surrounding her were comforting knotty pine, not high, impregnable red rock.

I must talk to Peter Rabbit, she thought, *tell him about my note to mother.*

Her eyes wandered to the queen's bouquet she'd hung above her mirror. The flowers were dried now, the baby's breath tiny white eyelets still lovely.

"Michelle Ann Strand," she whispered, "Joel said it was a beautiful name."

As soon as the family left next morning, Mickey hurried to the hatchery. It took her awhile to find Jim, but she did. He was beyond the bridge, on his knees, repairing a broken water main. He looked up.

"About yesterday, Jim—"

Jim put the pipe down and reached into his back pocket, pulling out a rag. He wiped his hands, then stood.

"I shouldn't have left you at the church the way I did, Mickey. It wasn't kosher, that's for sure. But I figured your boyfriend would give you a ride home."

A flush rose into Mickey's cheeks. She chose to ignore the last part of Jim's remark. "I'm not blaming you, Jim. I only wanted you to know that I understand."

Haltingly, stumbling over words, Mickey told him about her own reaction to the story of the prodigal son. She told him of her search for her mother that had resulted in an empty apartment in a run-down neighborhood.

"It would have meant a lot if I could have seen her, Jim, asked her face to face to forgive me, but I couldn't. I did leave her a note."

Jim was quiet for a long thoughtful moment, shifting the wrench from hand to hand. "But, Mickey," he said at last, "you went and asked for forgiveness. You tried to make things right." He laid the wrench beside the pipe, then slowly straightened. "Mickey, if you go away from your home, your people, the place you spent your childhood—even if you come back, do you ever really find it again?"

Mickey frowned, earnestness making little squint lines around her eyes. "I think in a way you'll be hunting for it all your life," she said. "I'm not sure. But if you find God—"

Jim reached out a grimy hand and patted her shoulder. "You're a good girl, Mickey. And I—I'm still nothing but a milksop." He shook his head. "I've no courage—no courage at all. And I'm afraid to trust God with my past."

With that incomprehensible statement, he turned and walked away. Mickey stared after him, then went back to the house.

After her morning work was finished, she picked up her Bible and went outside to the hammock beneath the birch trees.

This morning they were whispering, dipping and

swirling. *Like a maiden's fairness,* Mickey thought, *with those masculine dark firs towering protectively over them.*

Mickey lay in the hammock. The sun spangling through the leaves reminded her of the sequins that danced on the creek, shooting out miniature rainbows.

She opened her Bible and began to read the stories of the lost coin, the lost sheep and the lost son.

Her thoughts began to scatter, as spray against a heavy rock. She jumped as a glass pitcher swayed and fell, bursting into a thousand pieces.

"I didn't mean to waken you," Loretta said.

Mickey sat up. "You didn't." She remembered the bursting bottle. "I guess I was dozing a little. There was a pitcher breaking."

She rubbed her eyes, then looked up at Loretta; her face was white, her mouth worked helplessly. Mickey leaped to her feet.

"Loretta!" she cried, "what is it?"

Loretta sank heavily into a lawn chair and Mickey dropped to her knees beside her. Their hands clasped.

"I got a telephone call at work. Your mother—"

Icy coldness settled into the pit of Mickey's stomach. Her face drained of color, too.

"She's dead, isn't she—dead?"

Loretta nodded, tears filling her eyes. They trailed down her cheeks. *Like searing paths of pain,* Mickey thought.

But there were no tears in her own. They burned, like two fiery, unblinking stars.

"I'm so sorry, Mickey," Loretta whispered.

"Sorry?" Mickey hated the sound of her voice—

harsh, unfeeling. "Why are you sorry? She was *my* mother—"

She jerked her hands away. A part of her saw Loretta's startled hurt. But the other part?

"I think God's poison mean," she said ruthlessly. "Just when I was ready to love her—to care—"

She leaped to her feet, heard Loretta's wild cry, "Mickey! Come back! I need to tell you . . ."

But Mickey was running—away—away. The tall green firs opened their boughs and let her in.

Sixteen / Younger Sister

The hazelbrush slapped Mickey's arms. Overhanging blackberry vines clawed at her hair, twisted at her ankles.

Deeper and deeper into the heart of the woods she ran. The burning pain in her spirit turned into a searing pain in her lungs, her breath coming in ragged gasps.

She caught her foot in a vine maple crawling along the forest floor and went sprawling. Mickey didn't try to get up. She buried her face in the pungent green moss, her hands knotting into fists. Suddenly she was pounding the soft, yielding moss. "Oh, God!" she cried. "Oh, God." Even in her despair she thought of the tender moss being crushed, pummeled, beaten—like she was— "Oh, God!"

She rolled onto her back and looked up. The sunshine turned the color on the upper part of the tree trunks into shades of gray, from light to dark, accentuating the tiny moss clusters.

"God," she whispered, "couldn't you have at least let me say I was sorry?"

Bitterness rolled up inside her, holding back the tide of tears. "You're mean—poison mean, just like Jami said you were. Did it really mean so much to you, to take her just like that?"

There was a flash of blue high in the branches. Mickey closed her eyes. A bird trilled, a chipmunk scolded, a crow cawed from far away, the distance softening its harsh tones.

Slowly she became aware of a soft rustling around her. The vine maple leaves trembled in a stray breeze.

"Trust Me," they seemed to whisper. "Just trust Me."

Nearby alders took up the refrain. "Trust Me—trust Me—"

Then a new song, "I love you. I love you. I love you."

The pain dammed up inside Mickey's heart was suddenly released. "Oh, God," she cried through burning tears, "I love you. I trust you. Forgive me."

It was a weary, dirt-stained Loretta who found Mickey several hours later. Mickey, her head pillowed on the moss, lay fast asleep, the tear marks still on her cheeks.

Loretta sank down beside her. Her hands reached out, touching the tangled wispy hair. Tenderly she smoothed out leaves and twigs. "My little girl," she murmured. "My very own little girl."

Mickey stirred and opened her eyes. For a moment her dark eyes were peaceful. Then memory returned. "Oh, Loretta—"

Loretta's arms stole around her, gently holding her close. Mickey snuggled her face into her lap. The bushes resumed their gentle whispering—trust—love—trust—love. A woodpecker flew onto a maple limb and observed them curiously, cocking his head to one side.

"There's something I need to tell you, Mickey," Loretta said after a while. "Your mother—" She hesitated. "Your mother—was my sister."

Bewilderment furrowed Mickey's forehead. "I—I don't understand."

Loretta's lips quivered. "It isn't easy to explain, Mickey. So many things happened."

Mickey sat up and burrowed her face into Loretta's shoulder. "Tell me about it."

She felt Loretta take a deep, quivering breath. "It's a long story. But you—you need to know—

"There were just the two of us—Joanne and I. She was the older—so eager for life—so happy and alive. And I—I was the quiet one, the plain one who always had to wait for attention.

"I loved her, but sometimes it was hard—especially when she always seemed to get just what she wanted, then just as easily throw it away.

"She was that way with her men. Wanting them, then tossing them aside. And I—I couldn't even get one to pay me the least bit of attention—"

"You didn't need to," Mickey protested. "You had Kent."

A dark shadow flickered across Loretta's face. "This was before Kent.

"To make a long story short—we drew apart. I hated it when I heard she'd left you—to think she could take motherhood so lightly. It seemed so unfair! And always I was in her shadow—waiting for life—for love."

Mickey suddenly sat up straight. "You knew who I was," she cried.

"No, Mickey. I didn't know—not at first."

"But why didn't you tell me!"

"I didn't even tell Mrs. Morton! I was afraid being Joanne's sister might influence her. Because of Joanne's history, I wondered if I would be considered for your foster parent. And I—I wasn't taking any chances on losing you."

"But why didn't you take me right away—when Daddy couldn't, before I became a ward of the court?" Memories of her numerous foster homes flashed before her eyes: the endless round of new faces, new bedrooms, new schools—the voices, *"Mickey, you can't do that— we don't allow that. Mickey! Mickey! Why are you always running away?"*

"I lost track of you when Joanne left your father," Loretta replied. "I didn't know you didn't have a home! Not until I saw you with Mrs. Morton! No one ever told me!"

Mickey nodded. "They looked for my mother, too, and they couldn't find her either. They told me that once." She looked at the alder trees glinting golden in the slanting rays of sunshine. "Does Kent know I'm your real niece?"

"No. I never told him."

Loretta grew quiet, not seeming to want to talk any longer. Mickey noticed her fingers tightly clasped into fists—the dark circles beneath her eyes. Loretta had lost a sister. Maybe not a dearly loved one, but a sister just the same.

Compassion stirred in Mickey. She knew the hurt

that came when painful love twisted with regret deep inside the human heart.

She touched Loretta's clenched hand. "I'm so sorry, Loretta. To lose someone you loved long ago—grew up with—"

Tears misted Loretta's eyes. "Not as long ago as you think, my dear. I went back to the hospital alone, after I took you. I have you to thank for giving us those last weeks together."

She unclenched her fists and touched Mickey's cheek. "Joanne and I got to know each other—to understand. I even talked to her about you. She hung onto each word—"

A tide of bitter pain washed through Mickey. "Then how could you have let her be discharged to that awful place?" she whispered.

"I had to," Loretta murmured. "I had no choice—" She got up and held out her hand. "Come home, Mickey."

Home! A sweetness caressed her. Home! Mickey put out her hand and Loretta's own enclosed hers, drawing her to her feet.

"Loretta!" Mickey cried, sudden realization bringing wings to her voice. "You're my real aunt! My very own Aunt Loretta! And Kent' s my uncle—and Steve—"

Loretta's only answer was a quick squeeze to her hand.

That night when the house was quiet, Mickey thought about all that had happened to her in the past twenty-four hours. Yes, her newly-found Lord had allowed her mother to be taken from her, but He'd given her an aunt to love her, a lovely home by a magical stream that whispered and wooed, a church—Joel, Tam and—Peter Rabbit.

Mickey sat upright in her bed. "Jami," she whispered. "Jim. He's Loretta's stepson. That means—I have another cousin!"

She laughed out loud, hugging her knees with her arms. "My cousin—my friend—"

She hopped up and pulled out paper and pen from her desk drawer. The lamp burned late as Mickey's pen rolled across her paper.

She would tell Jami about her mother. She would tell him they were cousins. She'd ask him to come home—soon.

The day Joanne was buried was a golden day. The scent of flowers blew through the cemetery; the breeze wiped the cheeks of the mourners gathered beside the plain pine box.

The minister's words were few, his prayer simple. But, Mickey scarcely heard them. She stood beside her Aunt Loretta and thought how quickly the past dissolved into the future, and unfulfilled dreams were quietly laid aside.

Afterwards, a woman in a dress of puckered lavender put her hand on Mickey's arm. "You must be Michelle," she said softly.

Mickey looked at the round face filled with anxious concern, the gentle, childlike blue eyes.

"How did you know my name?" Mickey asked.

"Your mother told me about you. She was only in her apartment above me a few days before they took her to the nursing home. I found the note you left under the door. I thought it might be important, so I took it to the home. I read it to her that night—before she died."

The soft face crumpled. *She looks like a faded rose,* Mickey thought, *full-blown, petals about to fall.* Gently she put her arm around the drooping shoulders.

"I'm so glad you gave her my note," she said earnestly. "More than anything I wanted her to know I forgave her—that in spite of everything, I loved her."

The woman's lips quivered. "It meant a lot to her, I know. I'll never forget the way she clung to my hand and thanked me over and over . . . but I never dreamed it would be her last night."

Nor did I, Mickey thought. *Nor did I.*

She wandered over to the graves on the far side of the cemetery. An old tombstone without a name said: "God's lamb—The Lord took him." The lamb etched on the stone was filled with a soft green moss.

His mother rested close by: "Constance Harding—Christian, lady, mother."

Mickey's eyes smarted. A sudden movement in the field beyond caught her attention. She stepped around the sweet-scented lilac tree.

A man strode into the distance, his dark head held high. Mickey caught her breath. Peter Rabbit? But it couldn't be. He was far away bending over fish tanks, repairing water mains . . .

She opened her mouth to shout, "Jim," then shut it firmly. If he wanted to be near in her pain, yet unseen, that was his business. Vaguely she wondered if he'd ever met his Aunt Joanne.

Mickey reached for an aromatic lilac branch and breathed deeply. The man probably wasn't Peter Rabbit anyway.

Seventeen / The Whale

"This morning I'm noticing how often Abraham stood before his Lord—praying—listening," Mickey wrote. "I'm learning a little bit about that too—how to listen, how to pray."

Mickey stuck her pen behind her ear and smiled at the dancing cherry leaves surrounding her. Keeping a spiritual diary was becoming an important part of her life. It was something Mr. Hoffman had suggested she do.

Sometimes she wrote down a special verse, sometimes an observation or a thought that seemed important. Mickey liked the way it was helping change her.

Like the cherry tree, she thought, fingering her notebook. *First there are the blossoms, then the ripening fruit, and now green leaves drawing in sunshine, preparing for winter and another season . . .*

She turned to her new section entitled, NATURE. She had copied the idea from the old scrapbook Jami had left on the closet shelf. Stuffed with everything from animal track patterns to his own observations, it contained a wealth of information.

Already, her own notebook was filling with magazine clippings, observations from her daily woodland rambles, pressed flowers and leaves. It was always close by. Everyone in the family teased her about it, especially Kent.

"For a girl who hates school, you sure take the cake. Magazines—books—and *that* notebook." He'd gone off grumbling, but Mickey knew he was pleased at her interest.

Joel was too. Dinner on the River Queen had been a special occasion, a summer highlight, but rambling up and down the creek together, searching out crayfish, fingering beetles, bits of lichens—that had been the heart of the summer.

July had come with a bang from blazing fireworks at Oaks Park on the Willamette River with Joel, Tam and her boyfriend. It had gone out with glorious lightning ripping through giant thunderheads, thunder claps shaking her room.

It was August now with Queen Anne's lace decorating the roadside and white thistledown blowing high. Soon school would begin. In spite of the fears encasing her, paralyzing her with their strange hold, Mickey now knew she wanted to go.

She took a deep breath, anticipating autumn-hued sweaters, clubs and classrooms, football and cross-country and biology. Her fingers itched to curl around a microscope, explore the parts of a flower, peer into a bit of pond water . . .

But sometimes she wondered. Would the trauma of a new school, new classmates be worth suffering for the sake of activities and classes?

Occasionally she thought of her mother, but not

often. Only once had she been overwhelmed by her feelings. Tucked inside the pages of Jami's old scrapbook, she found a picture of her mother—young, happy, so very much alive.

Pain had stabbed her. A lonely cemetery, a dark-haired man in the distance, walking away. Jami's Aunt Joanne—her mother.

Mickey gathered her Bible and notebook together and moved to the window. Before climbing inside, she pushed a branch aside and looked at the hatchery.

Peter Rabbit—she knew something bothered him. She missed their comfortable comradery, their long talks. A pang shot through her. He'd been avoiding her.

She sensed it was more than his discovering her at his desk on that long-ago evening, when Steve had caught the poachers. Could it be the long letters she faithfully wrote Jami each week, the bits and pieces she shared about her new family?

Mickey dropped the branch and climbed in the window. As she smoothed her dark hair into place, she noted with satisfaction how her light blue shorts and blue-trimmed T-shirt accentuated her tanned arms and legs. Long, lazy hours on the whale rock and frequent dips in the stream were responsible. She smiled, her white teeth flashing against her dark skin.

She gave the girl in the mirror a smart salute, then gathered up swimsuit, towel and terry cloth jacket. She dashed downstairs.

"Steve!" she called. "Let's swim!"

The clock above the stove read 1:30. "He said we'd swim then," Mickey muttered.

She loitered for a half hour—folding scattered newspapers, replacing books on their shelves, tossing a withered bouquet of daisies and roses in the wastebasket.

Restlessness began to nibble at her. Could Steve have gone on ahead? She picked up her swimming gear and headed up the road, past the hatchery, to the stream.

The August sun was hot on her shoulders. In spite of her irritation with Steve, she was enjoying herself. The sun-baked earth, the occasional buzz of a fly were oddly comforting—perhaps because they went with long, sun-filled summer afternoons.

Steve was nowhere to be seen. The grassy meadow with the grill was empty, and the whale was bare.

Mickey slipped into the leafy glade, which served as a dressing room, and changed into her navy and white suit, and brief terry cloth jacket. Draping her towel over her arm, she went down the narrow path, across the small rocks, and up the whale head.

She spread her towel on the flat top of his head and lay down, the sun hot on her bare skin. She wished Steve would hurry.

The water lapped around the rock, whispering of delicious coolness, of crisp currents. Mickey stood up, went to the lower edge and ventured in an exploring toe. Ahh, this was the life.

She cast her jacket aside, lowered her foot, and began to wade into the deeper water. *I shouldn't,* she thought. *No one should ever swim alone.*

"Just once won't matter," she muttered. Quietly, the stream enticed her. A warm breeze, whispering, seconded the invitation. Gently the flow urged her farther and farther from shore. The cold water swirled around her shoulders; she was off and swimming, turning on her back, floating.

Suddenly, a sharp writhing pain clenched her stomach into a knot. Panic ripped through her. "Margot!" she cried. Then, "Help! Help!"

She tried desperately to keep her head above the water. But it was no use. The pain, mingled with the current, drew her down, down. A great burning filled her lungs. Then a darkness.

She was hardly aware of strong arms pulling her into the air. She gasped and choked. The rocky shore pressed into her side. A rough towel rubbed her dry. Then her terry cloth jacket covered her.

She opened her eyes. The trees wavered, then grew still. Jim's face came into focus.

His finger touched her cheek. "Don't cry, Little Bunny." But his admonition came too late. Mickey rolled onto her stomach, pressed her face into her hands, and let tears come.

Jim lifted her into his arms. "I'm taking you home."

Mickey didn't argue. She buried her face in his shoulder while weakness rolled through her in horrible sinking waves. A terrible trembling took control of her, and her teeth began chattering uncontrollably.

Jim hurried down the path, apologizing for the jouncy ride. But to Mickey it was the most wonderful ride she'd ever had. His steps were firm; his arms' tight hold radiated his caring. She knew Peter Rabbit was again her friend. His arms told her so.

He hesitated only once—at the gate. Loretta came running to open it, crying in a voice shrill with fright, "Mickey! Mickey!"

Steve followed her. "Is she all right?"

Kent came around the corner of the house. He quickly set down his shovel and motioned to the reclining lawn chair. "Put her here."

Gently, Jim laid Mickey in the lounger. Again he touched her cheek. "It's all right, Little Bunny. You're home now."

He turned to Kent. "I pulled her out of the whale hole up yonder. I think she stopped breathing for a bit—but she's all right now."

Loretta laid a blanket over her, tucking in the edges. "You need to warm up. I'll get you something hot to drink."

Mickey swallowed hard and looked at Kent and Jim. They just stood and stared at each other, neither one speaking.

She blinked hard. Did she see tears in Kent's eyes or just water in her own? She closed her eyes for a moment. When she opened them, Kent and Jim were in each other's arms.

Mickey knew she would always remember Kent's voice saying, "My son, my son. You've come home. Thank God, you've come home."

A delicious warmth stole into Mickey's heart. Then Loretta was in both men's arms, crying great heart-wrenching sobs.

Mickey understood. She clutched Steve's hand and pulled the bewildered boy close.

"He's their lost son—Jami—" she explained, "your brother."

But Steve shook his head. "How could he be?" he asked.

"He's Jami, grown," Mickey insisted. "I've known it for some time."

Steve scowled. "And you didn't tell me?"

"I didn't tell anyone."

"But Jami was a scaredy-cat, afraid of his own shadow! Peter Rabbit—Jim—is—" Pride shone in Steve's eyes. "Jim is a hero!"

Mickey closed her eyes. "Yes," she whispered, "Peter Rabbit is *my* hero."

Later that evening, Kent, Loretta, Steve and Mickey gathered in the living room. Mickey, warm and dry, snuggled in Kent's big, fuzzy, maroon bathrobe, was the center of attention.

"So you knew all the time!" Loretta exclaimed. "But how did you guess?"

"It started with the totem pole, and then the note."

"The totem pole?" Steve cried.

"What note?" Kent asked.

"I put it in the totem pole. It's there now."

Loretta flew up the stairs and brought it down. Mickey unscrewed it while Kent and Steve looked on. She laid the note on the coffee table. "I found it in back of the book shelves, wedged behind the baseboard. It said Spring Valley, so I started writing there.

"But it wasn't until I saw the letter I'd written to Jami on Jim's desk, the night Steve caught the poachers, that I knew for sure."

"He's grown that awful beard," Loretta exclaimed, "and he's taller and broader now. It makes me feel bad that I didn't recognize him."

"But you never saw him close before," Kent comforted. "If you had, you would have known."

"I'm not so sure," Loretta said. "He's changed. He's a grown man now—"

"A hero!" Steve exclaimed. "To pull Mickey out like that, bring her to shore—"

"He was afraid," Mickey said softly. "He told me so." She looked around the suddenly silent group. "He's blamed himself and hated himself all these years because of his fear of the water and what happened to Margot."

Kent nodded. "He told me he froze when he saw Mickey going off alone to the swimming hole. Then he said, 'But I had to follow her, had to face my fears once and for all.'"

He put his arm around Mickey. "If he hadn't, Mickey wouldn't be sitting here right now."

Steve's fingers traced the totem design thoughtfully. "I'm proud of my brother," he said, "proud of his carvings, his work at the hatchery. But most of all, I'm proud that he looked his fear in the face—and conquered it. Someday—"

Mickey lifted her chin expectantly. But Steve was silent. His "someday" would have to wait.

Mickey understood. Someday Steve would have to face his fear of heights—just as she would have to face her own fear—of school—of rejection.

She looked at Steve. Already, since she'd been here, he'd grown. His ankles stuck out awkwardly below his blue jeans. There was new purpose shining out of his blue-gray eyes. Mickey had a feeling Steve's someday would be soon.

That night Mickey lay in bed, too restless to sleep. The day's events whirled through her mind: the cold water sucking her down; Peter Rabbit rescuing her, carrying her home to her family . . .

Just before Jim had left, he'd pulled her aside. "I'm going to call Meredith," he had whispered, "tell her I've come home."

"I'm glad," she had responded. "She needs to know what I've known all the time—that you have courage."

An answering light had kindled in Jim's eyes. He had left walking tall, his dark head held high. Even now, Mickey could see him in her mind's eye.

Her door opened softly. Mickey turned her head, her heart scudding in sudden fear. Peter Rabbit? Had something happened? But it was only Loretta.

"Mickey," she whispered, "are you awake?"

"Yes." Mickey propped herself on one elbow. "What is it?"

Loretta came close to the bed. Mickey reached for the light switch, but Loretta's hand stopped her. "No," she said.

"Mickey, your mother asked me not to tell you something. But now—since Jami's return—your accident—I feel you have a right to know. That it would be important to you. I'm putting something here on your stand. After I leave, turn on your lamp. I think you'll understand.

Her fingertips stole to Mickey's cheeks. "We'll talk in the morning."

Then Loretta went out as softly as she'd come. Mickey waited until she heard the door close at the bottom of the stairs. Her fingers groped for the light switch.

Expectation filled her as she reached for the picture Loretta had left.

Mickey immediately recognized her mother and Kent. But the two children with them? She turned the picture over: Jami—age 6, Margot—age 4.

Mickey caught her breath as she bent over the portrait. Kent and her mother—both so happy, so young. Together.

Eighteen / Mother's Secret

Mickey looked at the cedar encircled enclosure; the spreading limbs before her formed a triangular opening partially blocked with a low-growing vine maple. Inside, a soft indentation in the earth marked the outline of a wild creature's body.

"Is this really a deer's bedding place?" Mickey asked, her voice tinged with awe.

Joel nodded. "Right there, that soft, hollowed spot. I like to call it 'Morning's nesting place.'"

Mickey lifted her head. "You think about her too, don't you?"

"And wonder. I guess I'll always think of Morning whenever I see a young doe. Maybe that's why it delighted me so—to find this."

"Morning's place."

"Yes, Morning's own place, if it is Morning's!"

"I think it is," Mickey said with quiet conviction.

"When I first found it early one morning, I touched it, and it was still warm. She must have just left." He held out his hand. "Shall we?"

Mickey nodded and started up the hill, then turned to look back. Mickey could imagine Morning's face peeking through the leaves, the flip of her white tail as she turned to run.

Farther along, the trees parted, and they hiked to the crest of a bluff. The hatchery, with its shimmering waterways, spread beneath them, soaking up the midday sun. The creek, slim and silver, rushed silently, muted by distance.

Quite suddenly Mickey understood why the stream had been named Eagle Creek. Remote, wild, holding inquirers just a little bit distant—yet wondrously beautiful and alive.

Mickey's face had turned rosy; her dark hair stuck to her temples with moisture. She stepped back into the shade of a giant fir and sat down flat, her legs stretching down the grassy slope.

She smiled up at Joel, pleased to have conquered the climb, but a little breathless, too. "What do you think?" she asked. "Would this make a nice picnic place?"

Joel looked around the clearing. "Except that we'd have to pack up water, it's perfect." He walked over to a bench-shaped boulder and sat down. "We could bring up a grill." He bent down, examining the rock. "There's a little hollow that goes way under. We could keep a coffeepot inside."

"And my totem pole on the top. I can imagine it sitting there—high above the creek."

"But the weather would ruin it," Joel protested. "It would get all cracked."

"I know," Mickey sighed. "It's only a dream. Actually, I'm going to keep it in my room always—to remember."

Joel slid off the rock and stepped over to Mickey, plopping down beside her. They were silent for a moment. A quail drummed somewhere in the woods; a bird close by gave a surprising little squawk; there was a faint humming buzz. The end of summer in all its fullness surrounded them.

"I went swimming with Steve yesterday," Mickey said.

Joel's brows quirked into a question. "And—"

Mickey leaned back into the warm sunshine. "It was special, Joel."

She sat up again, pulling her knees forward, wrapping her brown arms around them. "As soon as he asked me to go with him, I knew he had something on his mind. But it wasn't until we got to the whale that he told me.

"He asked me to just be there while he—he dove off the whale—alone." Her dark burning eyes sought Joel's. "He's afraid of heights, you know—

"Anyway, he asked me to cover my eyes. So I did. Except I peeked! Joel, he stood on that rock—trembling—afraid. Then he dove.

"There should have been bands playing. And cheers and pom-pom girls. But there was just me, and I wasn't supposed to be looking."

A proud glow filled her eyes. "He's different now, Joel. He looks his father in the eye and stands up straight."

"And Peter Rabbit—Jami—Jim—" Joel added. "He's different, too, since he pulled you out of the water."

Mickey nodded. She picked up a twig and began breaking it into little lengths, stacking them neatly. Joel began to lay them in the pattern of a little bonfire. He looked up.

"Mickey, something's changed you, too. And I don't think it was just Jami coming home."

Mickey nodded. "Loretta shared my mother's secret with me. That night, after I almost drowned, something happened that I haven't told anybody yet."

She took a deep breath. "Loretta came into my room and gave me a picture. It was a family portrait of Kent, my mother, little Jami and Margot—"

"What!" Joel exclaimed. His hand brushed the little bonfire into the earth.

"That's what I thought!" Mickey agreed. "The next morning Loretta told me the whole story. But first I need to tell you what Loretta told me when my mother died. She explained that Joanne was her older sister!"

"Sisters! Then that makes you and Jami cousins!"

"Wait—there's more. Years ago, before I was even thought of, my mother was married to Kent. Unwilling to handle her new responsibilities, she took off. I think from what Loretta said, Kent must have been a difficult husband, hard to please—"

Mickey shrugged. "Anyway, she left. Later there was a divorce, a lot of hurt and bitterness, and Kent alone with two small children. When Loretta offered to take them, Kent, not knowing how to care for them, was relieved. Loretta said she hated her sister for taking motherhood and wifehood so lightly. She had had everything Loretta had ever longed for and had merely tossed it aside.

"More and more Kent turned to her, and she grew to love him deeply. When he asked her to marry him, she was more than ready to say yes."

"But why wouldn't your mother have wanted you to know?" Joel questioned. "It doesn't make sense."

"That's what I said to Loretta! But when Mother was in the hospital, she begged Loretta not to tell me, that she was ashamed of the way she'd left both her families and deeply regretted it."

"But she took your brothers!"

"That's what I thought. But she couldn't keep them! Someday soon I'm going to talk to Mrs. Morton—see if I can find them. Mother confided in Loretta; she said the authorities wouldn't let her see them—because of the emotional scars she'd inflicted on their personalities."

Mickey's large brown eyes were deep wells of feeling. "Joel, do you know how wonderful it is to have the Lord? Someone you can count on always? Who'll never let you down?"

"Yes, but probably not in the same way you do. If one hasn't had real love—then when the real thing comes along—wow! Mickey, did Kent know?"

"No, not until Loretta told him—the same night she told me. Looking back, I can see that I reminded him of his Margot—our eyes and smiles are somewhat alike. But Loretta kept it all to herself—until Jami—"

"Jami! Why, Mickey, he's your brother!"

Mickey nodded. "That's why Loretta wanted me to hear the whole story. She felt I had a right to know—my own brother.

"I feel the Lord has given me a very special gift. All my life I've wished for a big brother. And Peter Rabbit—well—he's been that from the first, and I never even knew it. When I thought he was my cousin, I was delighted—and now to find he's even closer! It's one of those 'more than you ask or even imagine.'

"Ephesians 3:20. "Now to him who is able to do immeasurably more than all we ask or imagine, according to his power that is at work within us, to him be glory in the church and in Christ Jesus throughout all generations, forever and ever! Amen.' "

"And to think, I was sort of jealous of him—"

"You—jealous? Of Peter Rabbit?"

Joel grinned. "Oh, just a little. Sometimes I wondered. You seemed so close."

"We were—are." Mickey got up and walked to the edge of the bluff.

Her world lay before her, cradled in a giant cup. She almost wanted to stay here always—safe, protected, wrapped away from challenges.

But she couldn't. Jami had faced his fears, saving her—Steve had conquered his. Even Kent and Loretta were making peace with their past.

"Joel," she said, "I'm going back to school. I know it'll be hard, my being back a year and all. But I'm going."

Joel stood behind her, his hands clasping her tan arms. "But Mickey," he whispered, "you won't be alone. I'll be there."

His hands tightened. Mickey could feel his breath against her hair. "Mickey, I like to think you'll be there in the grandstands cheering me on, your cheeks pink in the cold, wearing a nubby blue sweater."

He stopped. Then, "Michelle Ann Strand, will you be my girlfriend?"

Mickey took a deep breath. Now she had a family, a Savior and Lord, and—a boyfriend.

She turned to him then. "Yes, Joel," she whispered, "oh, yes."